Ash

Di King

Published in 2011 by YouWriteOn Publishing

Copyright © Di King

First Edition

The author has asserted their moral right under the Copyright, Designs and Patents Act, 1988, to be identified as the author of this work.

All Rights reserved. No part of this publication may be reproduced, copied, stored in a retrieval system, or transmitted, in any form or by any means, without the prior written consent of the copyright holder, nor be otherwise circulated in any form of binding or cover other than that in which it is published and without a similar condition being imposed on the subsequent purchaser.

A CIP catalogue record for this title is available from the British Library.

Cover design by Debbie Harris

For: HH, JF, BW.

Ash
Geraldine — Ash's ex-wife
Tom — Ash's eldest son
Claire — Ash's middle daughter
Sasha — Ash's youngest daughter
Ali — colleague
Barry Petri — colleague
Renée — mentor
Eva — Ash's girlfriend
Rosemary — receptionist
Brett — gardener
Leila — trainee therapist

The Group:
Brenda
April Rose
Norma
Peter
Carl
Ronnie
Linda
Steph

Upstairs world:
Jessica
Drew

Chapter 1

Ash

The boy in the photograph looked serious. Shorts down to his knees, long-sleeved shirt and a sleeveless Fair Isle pullover. A long fringe contrasted with the shortness of the hair at the back. There had been a time when he'd religiously taken photographs, putting them into albums identifying them by year. Against each photo he would write a sentence or a word. It had given him great pleasure. He'd been a skilful photographer, taking care with light and composition. Now he didn't know if he could even find his camera.

Ash turned the page. He scrutinised the fading picture. Underneath in a thin hand was written 'Ashley's mother'. He pushed his glasses onto his forehead and peered at the picture but it was no clearer. No way of really seeing what she was like. Had Barbara meant him to find it? That sensitivity was not typical of his adoptive mother, but there was no chance of asking her now.

Standing up, he re-tied the belt of his dressing gown. He glanced at the clock. Taking a bottle of whiskey from the bow-fronted cupboard he poured himself a drink. He splashed in an equal measure of water from a jug. He put a log on the fire, placed the guard in front of it and went into the kitchen. He took a blue frying pan from the cupboard, poured in some oil from a spouted bottle and put it on the hob. He opened the oven door and stuck a knife into a potato, then lifted the peppered steak from the marinade and put it into the pan. It sent up a hissing cloud. He put the splash-tray over the steak and went back into the sitting room.

The faded face stared out of the page. Who was she? He sipped his drink. Not, who was she? He knew who she was but, *who* was she? What was she like? Would he have liked her? Would she have played with him? Coloured in drawings with him? Made cakes? And, always the unanswered question, why didn't she want him?

When Geraldine had told him she was pregnant, he'd been awed at the thought of being a father. It seemed such a huge thing. He re-read books with new understanding … bought more, modern texts with current thinking. He would give it, it was an it then and he didn't care if it was boy or girl, all the time in the world. They would play and have fun. It would be easy. You just give a child your time and your love. He would do it properly. He would show how it should be done. Not as it had been for him.

After the birth, Geraldine was so depressed and the baby was beautiful. A shock of dark hair and such blue eyes. Ash, watching them in the firelight, thought them the most beautiful sight. Geraldine, her hair loose, and the baby nestling reminded him of a painting he'd seen in a gallery in Stockholm. But she didn't want to be with the baby. Her mother arrived and, for once, Ash was grateful. Geraldine fed the baby for a few weeks, but with no pleasure and was pleased when the nurse suggested a bottle. She went through the motions of mothering and Ash took over many of the domestic chores. Gradually her depression lifted. Her mother visited less often and, greatly relieved at her return to health, Ash went back to fulltime work. They never talked about it and their lives developed a new routine. Then something he could never have imagined happened. He took against the baby. He hated its crying. The way the little fists pushed him away. The angry red face. How it preoccupied their lives. Horrified, he realised he was jealous and the baby didn't take to him. Even at the beginning, in the hospital, when the nurse put him into his arms, the baby had cried. When the same thing happened the next two or three times, he began to anticipate the crying and of course, it happened. His encouragement of Geraldine's bonding with the baby was partly because of his fear that neither the baby nor he wanted each other. Then, Geraldine broke her arm. A stupid accident. He took a month's compassionate leave. Now forced to look after the baby more, he pushed through the fist waving, the sick-ups and the rejection. At night Geraldine slept through but the baby did not. He took over the night-time feeds.

One night, grey with exhaustion from the crying, the baby fed, changed, burped but still crying, he felt tears welling up. He had no energy left. Spent, he sat on the edge of the bed. He looked down at the puckered face of his son and an overwhelming desire to shake and shake and shake him came over him. Almost roughly, he threw the baby onto the bed and walked to the window. He gripped his arms round himself, staying the trembling that seemed to come from his core.

Through the partially closed curtain, he saw the garden silvered by the three-quarters moon. Trees silhouetted in the light threw shadows across the elfin lawn. Light played on the rose arch that in the summer would be a tumble of fragrant blossoms. Stars shimmered and, in this vastness, he felt a peace. He returned to the distracted infant and picked him up. The baby gave an even louder cry. The infant's weight pressed into his arms and, in that moment, Ash saw a frightened, hurting little being, totally dependent. Gently holding the little fists down, he kissed the top of the hot little head. The crying stopped. Ash sat holding him, hardly daring to move. After a few minutes, the eyelids drooped and closed. Carefully he placed the baby in his cot and tucked the blanket around him. The baby gave a little whimper. Exhausted, he lay back on the bed, pulled the cover around him and slept till almost dawn.

From that moment a love developed, so deep that it startled him. Now Tom no longer cried when he saw him but brightened and gurgled, holding out his arms and Ash felt a love for this little creature that he had never felt for another human being. He never confessed, even to Geraldine, his fears and revulsion in those first months and he soon forgot those shameful feelings. By the time Tom was walking, he and Ash were inseparable. He couldn't imagine ever giving a child away.

The timer on the cooker beeped with high-pitched insistence. What had happened to his mother to make her give away her baby? He stood up. He placed the thin shiny paper over the page and shut the album.

Chapter 2

April Rose

Ash pulled the door to and pocketed the key. Leaves scattered the lawn and made imprints on the path. Bending down he picked up a shiny red leaf. He twirled it in his fingers as he walked to the car. In the car he put a letter and the leaf on the passenger seat. The familiar postmark confirmed this letter's origin. One good thing to come out of all this was that Tom now wrote letters.

He turned in between the stone pillars of 'The Firs' and eased his convertible into his designated space. Barry Petri's silver Jag was already there. He picked up the letter. As he opened his door he just touched the Jag. He couldn't help a smile.

There was no one on reception. Yesterday's anemones in the pink vase looked sad. He walked towards the stairs and pausing by the landing window saw a blue Astra turn into the car park.

In the office he crossed to the window and opened it. The garden was rich with autumn colour. He loved this garden and wondered that so few of the patients and almost none of his colleagues seemed to appreciate it. He took off his jacket and put it on the back of the chair. He put the letter on his desk and took his diary from the drawer. He had a meeting at eleven but before that he was seeing Peter Tavener and a new patient, April Rose, who'd been referred for his Tuesday group. He glanced at this watch. Eight thirty. Barry's briefcase was on his desk. He would be in the cafe. He wondered whether Barry told his wife that he had a second breakfast when he got to work. He pulled April Rose's file towards him. He took his pen from his briefcase and wrote the date on a piece of paper. There was the usual information, name, address. She was twenty-five. Same age as Tom. He turned the page.

> *The patient presented with severe loss of identity, describing herself at times as 'feeling like a gas', unboundaried, no edges, walking invisibly through*

crowds, passers-by only aware of a slightly unpleasant odour as she passed...

Ash put down his pen. He took off his glasses and leaned back in his chair. It was going to be unusually hot again. In the distance he could hear the sound of a drill. They were still working on the reception area. He glanced at the clock. Five minutes. He picked up his pen.

April was not in a good state. On a scale of one to ten she would say she was four. The room was quite nice, she thought. Big and airy. Her heart was beating fast. What would Dr A Jones be like? He would certainly be either patronising or disinterested. She didn't care. She didn't have to be here. He did. This was his work. She thought about that for a moment. He had to be interested in her. He would arrive with a file. Words written about her and they would all be wrong. They all thought they understood her but they didn't even begin.

She felt hot, dirty and ugly and her skirt felt too short. She couldn't remember if she'd done her hair this morning. She certainly hadn't put on any make-up? Her heart was racing now. She had to look. She'd noticed a toilet by the door where she came in. She picked up her bag, grabbed her cardigan and turned to the door.

'Good morning, April. I'm Dr Jones.' She sank back into the seat. She felt caught out, exposed. It wasn't fair. Why hadn't he let her go and look in the mirror? He was early. It was probably a trick. To make sure she didn't have time to go to the toilet and see if she were all right.

'You found it all right?' he said.

How did he know? In the end she'd asked the man with the dog and he'd walked with her to the end of the road. Three minutes of agony as they walked along together. Everybody knew what this place was for. The dog was old with matted fur and sores so he had nothing to be superior about but she had to be nice because he was being kind.

'... the group ... on a Thursday,' Dr Jones said. 'You didn't hear what I said. You seem uncomfortable. Is this making you feel nervous?' She stared past him. 'April. You don't have to tell me anything today that you don't want to.' They always said that. She'd end up saying things she hadn't meant to and then it was out the door, goodbye and she never saw them again and they had all that information about her in their heads.

Dr Jones had put his notebook down. He was leaning back in his chair. He smiled.

'What was it like … coming here today?' he asked.

'OK.'

'How long since you were in hospital?'

'Seven weeks,' she said. It was all in her notes if he bothered to look. But he wasn't looking at them. It was like they were just talking.

'I had a little dog once,' Dr Jones said. 'He was called Mustard. He came to live with me when he was about six months old.' April stole a glance at him. Why was he talking about his dog? 'He was affectionate and playful,' Dr Jones continued, 'and he seemed happy, most of the time. That was until any stranger came to the door. Then he would snarl and growl and twice he bit somebody who tried to get near him.' Dr Jones paused. 'I wonder if you sometimes feel a bit like Mustard. Scared. Not sure if you can trust people.'

'Sometimes I feel like a gas wafting through the streets,' April began. 'Nobody sees me … I am invisible.' He didn't laugh. He listened. She wished she could reach out her arms to him. Sink into the warmth and comfort. Put her head against his solid chest. Tears prickled. She stood up.

'You're all the same,' she said. 'You can't help me. You don't understand me. What do you know about being me?' In a stride she was across the room. The door slammed violently, shuddering the flowers in the vase.

Ash was shaken by April's abrupt exit. Even on this short acquaintance, he had made up his mind to offer her a place in his Tuesday group and this was disappointing. Had he been too gentle, too tough, not direct enough, too … anything?

In his office, a tray with coffee had been placed on his desk. He drank the coffee and ate two chocolate biscuits instead of his usual one. When he'd finished, he picked up the tray and placed it on the table outside the office. At his desk, he took the letter out of his briefcase and opened it slowly. The familiar backward writing and Birmingham address confirmed the sender.

'*Thursday 23rd* he read. Even now the austere address and number gave him a jolt.

> *Dear Dad,*
> *I hope you are well. Thanks for your last letter. Mum says you are coming to see me on the next visit. I've booked it and she says will you confirm that you are going otherwise she will come instead. Last week they moved me to a new wing. It means I have to share with a different bloke. He seems OK. They don't give you any notice. You just get told. It means I can do more work. That's why they move you. It's not so far for them to fetch you. It's not mailbags but nearly as tedious. At least it gets me out of the cell. I am working my way through all the books in the library, when it's open. You would be appalled if you could see the limited collection but I just read anything. I'm into self-help books this week ... funny that. Some are quite good. Mum came last time when you couldn't get here. She looks tired. I wish you two would talk. I'm going to all sorts of groups. I think it's ironic. I just sign up for everything. It is hard to stay motivated so it helps. It would be really good to see you Dad. Let me know if you can make it.*
> *Love Tom*

Ash put the letter down. How had it come to this? Every time he got a letter. Every time Geraldine phoned. Every time he read an article or heard a programme about prison, he felt the same. If you do wrong you should be punished. He believed that, but not his son. Tom was no criminal. He'd gone off the rails, but he wasn't bad. He should have opened the letter later. He had Peter to see in a few minutes. It was all down to parenting, how often he'd said it. He saw evidence of it every day; this was no different. Just above his temple he felt the throbbing. Please don't let his neuralgia start. He must make time to see Renée. He needed to talk. In the corridor a door banged. He put the letter back in the envelope and put it carefully in the pocket of his briefcase.

It would be really good to see you Dad. His throat was tight. He went over to the filing cabinet and found Peter Tavener's file. Slipping his jacket over one shoulder, he picked up the file and his briefcase and left the room.

Chapter 3
Jessica

Delicate light blurred harsh outlines. Jessica reached out to touch a wispy cumulus. She moved through arches of white jasmine. She bent to smell a petal, and disturbed a white butterfly fanning gently. Beside the path a fountain played water into an open shell and a bird trilled, lark-like. It was all warmly familiar to her but today, when there would be new returnics, she viewed it as they might. Warm air held her at a temperature that completely matched her own, and, glancing down she saw her strongly beating heart, beautiful in its detail.

She looked up as a white hare ran across the path and stopped. Ears pointing, it raised itself on its hind legs, sniffing the air. At her movement it bounded into the distance, leaping high, fading before it was out of sight.

Ahead was the barn ... high doors which opened as she approached. Pale wooden beams criss-crossed under a high roof. Soft music played. She walked through the hall to a row of doors. She knocked gently on one of the doors and walked in. Two men sat at desks. Jessica walked over to the older of the two men and touched him lightly on the shoulder.

'How's it going?' she asked. The man pushed himself back from the desk.

'There's a lot this week,' he said. 'Do they know how complicated it is?' Jessica smiled.

'Sorry Drew but here's another.' He made a face. 'This family needs a boy and she needs to have older siblings.' Drew sighed. 'It's OK apart from that.'

'But I haven't got anyone else – not who can cope with the mother.' He clicked a key and they both looked at the screen. He tapped the computer keys. The young woman put a hand on his shoulder.

'What if you left her until next week? The parents aren't panicking yet ... then you could put her,' she tapped the screen, 'in here. She'd

be one of seven then and that mother will give her all the stress she needs.'

'You're a genius, Jess,' said Drew. 'I could kiss you.'

'Better not,' she said.

Jessica Long left the room and walked back along the corridor to her department. She sat down and pressed a switch. The huge screen filled with arrows and circles. With the cursor she added the name to a list of names on the right of the screen. A smaller screen replicated the alteration. She clicked on the save key.

Chapter 4
Brenda

It was hot in the reception office. The winter heating had been turned on, and this beautiful autumn day could not be legislated for; the timer had been set. Two women occupied the five-desk room. The older woman wore a neat blouse and skirt and her shoulder-length hair, secured with an Alice band, suggested that her style had not changed since her student days. At the other desk, Brenda tapped at her keyboard, every so often stopping to bite at a piece of skin on her finger. The phone on her desk rang. She tutted and lifted the receiver. She listened for a few seconds.

'OK. I'll tell him ... Yes ... I'll tell him. I said I'll tell him!' Rosemary looked up. 'He's taking a group. I can't disturb him now ... I can't help it. I've told you.'

'What's the matter?' asked Rosemary. Brenda put her hand over the mouthpiece.

'It's Stuart what's-his-name. Wants to speak to Dr Jones.' She put the phone back to her ear. 'Yes. I said I will ... oh sod off.' She banged the receiver back on the cradle.

'Brenda ...?'

'I can't bear it. I'm only doing my job.' Brenda started tapping furiously. 'The nutters are so bloody rude.'

'But what did he want?'

'To sodding speak to Dr Jones ... I told him he can't.'

'Did you tell him to phone back?' said Rosemary.

'No I bloody didn't.'

'Don't you talk to me like that,' Rosemary said, getting up.

'Oh shut up. Just shut up,' Brenda snapped two tissues from the box in quick succession. She put them to her eyes and then blew her nose.

'Brenda, what's the matter?' Rosemary asked.

'You are ... they are ... all of you ... I hate the lot of you ... and I hate you and your soddin' egg sandwiches!' Brenda was shouting now. 'Every day at twelve twenty, out come the egg sandwiches and I hate the smell. Makes me want to be sick. Every day. Twelve twenty. Egg sodding sandwiches!' The door opened. Ash stood in the doorway.

'What's going on? I'm trying to run a group next door.' Brenda wheeled on him.

'And you can piss off too. They all want to talk to you. Well they can't. They bloody can't.'

Chapter 5

Tom

'Ash?' Geraldine's tone was petulant. 'Can you do this Wednesday ... Tom's visit? Claire's found this amazing dress and she wants me to go and see it.'

'But I was going next week. I've taken the day off.'

'You can change it, can't you? I don't want to let Claire down.'

'I've got patients. I can't just ...'

'You've always got patients. It's always the same. Your family comes last.'

Ash sighed. This was familiar territory. He moved the phone to his other ear. He was rapidly calculating whether he could cancel his Wednesday list.

'OK. One of us must go and if you feel Claire's dress is more important.'

'Don't say it like that. I just think we should share it and I've done the last two visits.'

'Yes. OK, I'll phone and see if that's OK.'

'Good. Bye.' Her phone went down immediately. No chat. No question. Before she phoned Geraldine would have already made up her mind.

He hated cancelling. It was messy. People waited so long for an appointment. But Rosemary obligingly cancelled all but the new person. He'd have time to see her. The journey usually took him about two hours. If he left by ten he could be on the motorway by half past.

He opened the wardrobe. He chose a neatly ironed lilac shirt and the striped tie that Tom had given him one Christmas. He needed to be smart this morning but he could take his tie off when he got there, so he would feel less like an official visitor. It felt trivial to be thinking about what to wear, but it kept him grounded to think about the mundane. Before he left the flat, he washed up and tidied the sitting room, putting the magazines and papers that he'd strewn across the table into a neat pile and plumping up the cushions on the sofa. The freesias and lilies in the glass vase smelt and looked lovely. He pinched off a dead flower. Anybody coming in would not judge him, single man living in squalor.

It was nearly ten. The patient had been late. Back in his office, Ash picked up his briefcase, checked his car keys and walked toward the door. The door opened and Barry Petri dashed in.

'Ah – Ash. I need a word.'

'Sorry Barry. I'm in a rush. I'm in early tomorrow.' Barry looked agitated.

'No – sorry. I must sort this out. It won't take long. It's about ...'

'I've got to go. Sorry Barry.'

'I'm sorry Ash.' He was almost barring the way. 'This must be sorted out today.' His tone was insistent.

'OK. But it must be quick.' Ash rested his case on the desk but did not sit down.

'It's about Brenda Chit.'

'Oh – surely that can wait.' Ash picked up his case.

'No. It can't. There's been a development. She needs to have an assessment. It's complicated. You know she was on probation.

'No. I didn't, but why can't you assess her?'

'Like I said, it's complicated.' Ash raised an eyebrow at his pedantic colleague's mistake. 'You're the only one who can do it. Besides, she'll talk to you.'

'What about Ali? Can't she do it?'

'No, she can't,' he snapped. 'Besides she can't stand her. No, it'll have to be you.'

'Look, Barry. I'm not sure she will talk to me either. What's it about? No, tell me tomorrow. I really must go.'

'So you'll see her?'

Ash reached in his briefcase for his diary. 'What am I assessing her for anyway?'

'She might agree to join a group.'

'Not here!'

'Well – no – it wouldn't be ideal, but well – my hands are a bit tied.'

'I've got a space at nine thirty. Now Barry, I really must go.'

'Good. Thanks. I'll tell Rosemary to book it.'

The door opened, nearly knocking into Petri, Ali walked in.

'Hello. Am I interrupting something?'

'No,' said Barry quickly. Ali walked towards her desk. A delightful waft of perfume followed her.

'What's the conspiracy?' she said over her shoulder. Petri looked towards Ash, indicated towards her and put his finger to his lips.

'Hum … very mysterious,' said Ali. Barry followed her out and was at the bottom of the stairs before Ash reached the end of the landing.

The traffic on the motorway was moving steadily and he settled back to enjoy the drive. The countryside was wintry and beautiful. Birch trees stood out with sculptured delicacy against the blue-grey skyline. Tractors ploughed the fields into parallel order. He needed to think about Tom and what he might tell him, but the conversation with Petri kept nagging at him. He changed the channel to Radio Three. A tortured piece, all discordant notes, jarred his thoughts. Radio Four was nature. He turned off the radio. He was bored with the CDs. Why was Barry so insistent and why did he want Brenda Chit assessed at 'The Firs'? There was no way she could be treated there. Not while she was working there. Why had Petri set it up and, what was much more disturbing, why had he agreed to it? It wouldn't do. When he got back, or if he had a moment today, he would phone Barry and say he had changed his mind.

He turned into the car park and thankfully parked in the one place left overlooking the river. He had ten minutes to spare. The river was running quite fast and the usual debris had been moved down river, making it more attractive than usual. A group of ducks bobbed with the flow. He locked the car and walked quickly towards the gates. He wondered if he cut it fine so he didn't have time to think, little time to take in the castle-like exterior of the prison, the wooden gates, the bell. He produced the authorisation letter and was let in. He crouched through the doorway, and crossed the yard. A woman in a mac hurried in front of him. He went through the next gate, showing the letter again. Uniformed, burly officers, polite but bored.

'Put your phone, keys and any valuables into the locker please, sir. You can take some small change for the drinks machine.' He stood while they searched him and looked up at the camera as instructed. 'Open your mouth please sir.' He felt humiliated and dirty, each action stripping away a little of his identity. How much more so, if he didn't know that in an hour he could leave. How had Tom borne it? He joined the group of visitors by the glass doorway. He nodded to a man he had seen before but most kept their eyes down. A young woman carried a child.

The first glass door opened and six people were counted in. The rest waited while the six were momentarily imprisoned in the glass cage. They were let out at the other side and six more went in. Ash counted how many were left. He didn't want to push in but he wanted this bit over. After another lot, he was counted in. For what felt like a long minute, they were held between the two glass doors. On either side people moved back and forth. He started to sweat. With a faint hiss, the doors opened and they were walking down the corridor, their feet making a dull rhythm. An officer opened the door and they filed in.

Around the room people sat in pairs either side of low tables. The prisoners in tee-shirts, jogging-bottoms and tabards. He panicked. He couldn't pick Tom out in the sea of grey. Officers stood or leaned against the walls. Streams of light shone in parallel shafts from high windows. Adjusting his eyes he scanned the room. At that moment Tom stood up and Ash approached the table. His six-foot frame looked thinner than on the last visit and his hair, always a bit tousled, looked dull and tangled. But, most shocking was his face, taut and gaunt under the initial smile, and his eyes, dull and dark.

'Hi Dad. Good to see you.' They hugged warmly but broke off self-consciously as an officer indicated for them to sit.

'It's good to see you too.' They sat for a moment looking at each other. Ash reached out to touch his arm, swallowing to control brimming tears.

'You got my letter?'

'Yes, thanks. How are you? What's happened about the library? Have you got enough to read? I don't know why they won't let us bring you books. I spoke to your mother. She sent her love.' He realised he was gabbling and that twice he'd interrupted Tom. He took a breath and slowed down. He felt out of place and childish as if Tom, with his grave eyes, was the adult. There was an awkward silence. There was so much he wanted to say.

'They've moved me.' Ash nodded. 'I'm sharing with this new guy. He's OK. We don't bother each other.' Tom was looking directly at him. A look that conveyed relief and something else. Fear. Ash's heart lurched.

'I guess it makes a difference ... who you share with.' Tom nodded.

'It does. I hope they don't move me again. This man's OK.'

Suddenly there was a loud noise. Tom jumped violently. A man with a cap bent to pick up the dropped walking stick. Tom flashed a rueful smile.

'How is it Tom? How are you managing?'

'Well — you know. I'm managing ... but it's pretty awful.' He lowered his voice. 'I just count the days and keep my head down and I'm so bored.' Tom looked at his hands. 'There's this education thing though. I'm doing IT stuff but the classes get cancelled all the time. I wake up in the morning and I can't believe I'm here.'

'Tom. I'm so sorry. I can't imagine what it's like. I think it's amazing that you've survived so well. How are you managing with ... without the drink?'

'OK.'

'At least there's no temptation in here.'

'I could get it if I wanted it.

'What?'

'You can get anything in here ... if you want it.' Ash frowned. 'Don't worry Dad. I don't want any. I really have learned my lesson and ... I'm going to all the AA meetings. My name's Tom and I'm an alcoholic.' He gave a weak smile. Ash did not smile back.

'Can you sleep?'

'Oh ... you know. Not like at home.' Tom looked down and Ash realised how difficult this must be for him and some instinct told him that for once, making light of things might be for the best.

'Your mother's gone with Claire to look at a dress. An amazing dress, as she put it.'

For the first time Tom gave a smile. 'Good old Claire. It would have to be amazing for her. Mum will like that.'

A bell jarred right through him, announced the end of visiting time. Ash got up reluctantly and hugged Tom again.

'Can you come next week?' Tom looked tall and lost and alone. Ash hesitated.

'I'm not sure. I'll try,' he said. 'If not your Mum will. She might bring Claire.'

'Is Claire all right about it?' Ash hesitated.

'I'm sure she is. One of us will come. Take care Tom.' How inadequate that sounded. 'We're all thinking of you.'

'Thanks, Dad,' said Tom.

Ash drove home, pensive and glum. Halfway home, he realised that he was longing for a drink and that he would have one when he arrived home. How did that make him any different from Tom? Because he could resist if he wanted to. Or thought he could. Not tonight though. Tonight the craving was insistent. How much control did he have? Does it affect your life style? He functioned. Yes, he had the occasional hangover if he'd been out drinking with Ali, but it was the exception rather than the rule. An image of the cut-glass decanter on his sideboard, the click of the glass, swam into his mind. There was no doubt it was a regular habit. Turn the key. Open the door. Hang up his coat. Put on his slippers and … pour himself a whiskey. Was alcohol a regular part of your family life when you were growing up? What would Tom have answered?

Heavy rain started and he turned on the wipers. Visibility was poor and lorries threw up cascades of spray. He realised that under the love and the guilt, he was also angry. Deeply, hurtfully angry with Tom. Hadn't they done enough? When did you ever get let off the hook as a parent? How did that tousle-headed engaging little boy, full of questions and interest, turn into that surly teenager, rejecting their love and interest. That stage had at least been understandable. But the nasty, unkind young man that was once his son, loafing about and tanked up with cannabis and alcohol, how had that happened? All his knowledge and experience was no use in the face of the hostile, vicious rejection. Tom had parents, love and interest; how could he be so ungrateful? A blue car shot past in the outside lane. He must be doing ninety. Ash checked his speed. What had made Tom go off the rails? Something did. Something was missing. The drugs and the drink compensated for something. Did it all stem back to Sasha? Had Tom felt, under the sadness, that he was neglected? Each of them huddled in their own grief. And they had been close, Tom and Sasha. Of course he took it badly. Claire weathered it better, or appeared to. But then, she was a different sort of person, older, self-contained. Tom was the sensitive one.

He turned off the motorway and followed a van with the slogan 'Let us move you' onto the slip road. Sasha was the happy one, bright and full of energy. Did he still underestimate how it had affected Tom? Each in their own way struggled through the guilt. Should she have been out playing? The truth was that it was sometimes a relief to have a break from her energy and questions?

'Yes, darling. You and Tom go and play for a little while.' Should they have done something about the cars parked too close? Why was she out in the street anyway? Where was Tom? Couldn't he have kept an eye on her? Their belief in the idea of letting children have some freedom. Not cooped up indoors all the time. How he wished now that she had stayed cooped up and ... here.

'*Daddy, come and see my lettuces. They've got tiny leaves.*' She loved the garden almost as much as he did.

He looked at the dashboard clock. It was three o'clock. What was Tom doing now? Locked in his cell. Hoping he and the other man would not irritate each other too much. Anticipating the next meal. Hoping there would be no trouble; that he wouldn't be picked on. Sudden anger welled up again. All those people advocating tough love. They didn't know how hard it was when it was your own child. Resisting the pleading phone calls. Knowing he was probably sleeping in his car or on the floor of some cruddy room. Then the police on the doorstep. Drunk driving. Damage to several cars in a Tesco's car park. Nobody hurt. An older couple a bit shaken by the abuse.

It was a terrible shock, but there was an awful resignation. It had all gone on for so long. There'd been so many chances. So many promises. Then bail and that could have been the end of it, but it wasn't the end. Like a moth drawn to a flame. Tom had sealed his own fate in not turning up for that bail hearing. Where had he been? Drunk somewhere? Sleeping it off?

He braked, changed gear sharply and pulled out to overtake a cyclist. And that was it. Had they wanted to make an example of him? Who knows? The shock on his face. Looking to them imploringly as he was led away. No goodbye. Gone. The impotence he felt. It couldn't be happening. Wanting to turn to Geraldine. She, unsmiling, managing. On the steps, she allowed a hug. A moment of bewildered shock but they were already beyond helping each other. Too much had happened. Over the phone, they made practical arrangements and when Tom applied for visiting rights, Geraldine did the first visit. It didn't work for them to go together and being so far away, it meant Tom had more visits.

The rain was easing. Deep puddles lined the road and waterlogged fields stretched away to the right. Would it be worth it in the end? It certainly couldn't go on. Had Tom really reached rock bottom or would he just get through it and start again? Tom, always too gentle to use his height and strength to hurt anybody, but Tom who also had a temper. He hoped he wouldn't be too provoked. It was all wrong. He suddenly felt so weary and defeated. He parked and walked the short path to the flats. As turned the key in the lock, he realised he hadn't phoned Barry Petri about Brenda Chit's assessment.

Chapter 6
Assessment

At nine twenty-five Barry was still not in so Ash had no chance to speak to him. He still hadn't appeared at nine thirty so Ash went down to the group room. Brenda was already in there sitting by the window. He fetched a high-backed chair and placed it near the sofa. He pulled over a second chair to put his case on. He felt she was watching him and enjoying his discomfort. He sat down and reached in his briefcase for his glasses. The case fell out and burst open sending his glasses skidding under the chair. He retrieved them awkwardly. He took a breath and tried to settle himself. He felt strangely intimidated.

'So Brenda ... you know why we are meeting today.'

'Dr Petri says I've got to join a group.'

'What do you think about that? Do you want to join a group?'

'No, not really.' She seemed softer today, more reflective.

'Have you been in a group before?' he asked.

'Yes ...'

'When was that?'

'When I was ... you know ... in hospital.'

'That was when?' Ash reached for her notes, allowing her a chance to elaborate. He had read her notes briefly this morning.

'Is that my file? Have I got a file?'

Ash smiled. 'We've all got a file Brenda. Mine's probably thicker than yours.' Brenda gave a quick smile.

'I was in Meadow Lane two years ago, for four months and three days.'

'Was that your choice?'

'I don't know why I have to do this,' Brenda said suddenly. 'I don't need any more therapy. There's nothing wrong with me now and if I've got problems, I talk to my friends about it.'

'Does that work?' said Ash.

'Sometimes, but sometimes they're busy ... or they don't listen. Dr Jones, I don't want to join a group. It's Rosemary, isn't it? I bet she's been complaining.'

'Why would she complain about you?'

'I get angry sometimes. I was angry with Stuart Bessel last week and Dr Petri said I've had a lot of time off, but I get ill. Everybody gets ill.'

'What sort of ill?'

'I get a bit down sometimes.'

'Is that when you get angry?'

'Yes … the clients always want something. They're lucky to have this place but they're always ringing up, wanting to talk to … all of you. It isn't fair. You're busy. They ought to have more respect.'

Brenda held her hands in her lap and sat forward on the settee as she spoke. Not having given her much attention before, he now saw an almost attractive young woman in her thirties, thirty-four actually, he'd seen in her file. She had a nice complexion, he noticed, and rather surprising green eyes. She'd stopped talking and was looking at him.

'You have a sister, don't you?' he said. 'Are you close to her?' Brenda shook her head.

'No, she's up in Stoke. I only see her if I go up there. She never comes to see me. I've got a brother too, but he's in Scotland.'

'What about your parents?'

'Mum's dead. I never see my dad.'

'Nobody else? No other family?' She shook her head. 'That sounds quite lonely.' A look crossed her face, sad but something else as well. 'Wouldn't it be good to have other people to talk to who are coping with the same sort of things as you?' he asked. In an instant, the look changed to the familiar, hard look that he had sometimes noticed when she was on reception.

'Look. I don't need therapy. I told you. I've done all that. I'm better now. It isn't fair. I do a good job here. I've got much better computer skills than Rosemary and I'm the only one who can read Mr Dare's writing. It's discrimination. If I'm asked to leave, I will go for unfair dismissal. There's things I could say about this place.'

'What do you mean?' Ash asked.

'Doesn't matter, but I know my rights.' Ash paused for a moment.

'Look Brenda. I'll put my cards on the table. As far as I understand, Dr Petri is concerned about how you are with your colleagues and the patients, and your absences. You're on probation, and if things don't improve, you are likely to be asked to leave. It isn't about the quality of your work, just your interaction with people. Now I think there are reasons why you sometimes get angry. However, if you can't get it under control, you are in danger of losing your job. I am suggesting that if you join a group and work at your anger, you not only keep your job, but you might start to feel happier.' He paused. 'Now that was quite a speech. What do you think?' Brenda seemed to be thinking but said nothing. Well, I've tried, Ash thought. Barry will have to take it from here and, he glanced at his watch, he needed to finish now. Brenda sat looking at her hands. It was very quiet, he noticed. No drills. No movement in the corridor. In the sunlight he saw that the room looked a bit shabby. It would be good when they started re-decorating the building.

'Would I have to come to the group every week?' Ash looked up.
'Well ... yes.' Brenda nodded.
'What if I was too busy?
'You'd be given time off.'
'What day is it?
It'll probably be the Friday group at Fairfield's.'
'Not here then?'
'No.'
'How would I get there?' Ash raised an eyebrow. 'Yeah. Bus, I suppose.'
'What are you thinking? Are you willing to try?'
'OK. The people in your group seem to think it helps.'
'OK Brenda. Good. I'll let Dr Petri know.'

Almost as soon as he got to his office, Barry appeared.
'How did you get on?'
'A bit tricky but I think I've persuaded her to go to the Fairfield's group if she can go on a voluntary basis, initially anyway.'
'Do you think she'll go?'
'Don't know. Now perhaps you can tell me what this is about. If she's on probation, why can't we just sack her if she's no good? Has she been that difficult?'

'She's getting impossible, Rosemary says. She's rude in reception and she's always taking time off. She's a good secretary though and on a good day, when she's well, she's quite likeable, apparently.'

'So what's the problem?'

'The problem is, Richard has no real grounds for dismissing her and she was the union rep at her last place and she knows all the procedures. And ... she's threatened to make a complaint against Ali.'

'About what?'

'Not really sure ...' Barry looked uncomfortable.

'Richard doesn't want a fuss and I don't want to lose Ali. Brenda's clearly got problems but ... we knew that when she was taken on. Rosemary quite liked her at the beginning. She likes people with a bit of history. She thinks they're good here, they understand. Remember Sally, she was brilliant.'

'Yes, but she'd had lots of therapy.'

'Exactly. I thought if Brenda would have some help, we could keep her on here and not have to go through the dismissal thing ... and risk a complaint. The trouble is she knows the ropes.' He stood with his hand on the door handle.

'I'm glad she's agreed to the Fairfield group. Thanks. I'm quite surprised though. She told me she would only join one of your groups.'

Ash went cold. Christ. Had she understood that it would not be his group? Had he made it clear? He recalled her words ... people in your group seem to like it. Had she thought that he was interviewing her for his group? Another muddle. No, she must have understood. Well if she hadn't, Barry would have to sort it out.

Chapter 7
Ali

Ali lit a cigarette. She smoked with great relish inhaling deeply then exhaling, head slightly averted from him. She always wanted to meet here where she could sit outside with the other smokers in relative comfort. Later he would find the smell on his clothes unpleasant.

'Don't look now here comes one of yours,' said Ali looking over his shoulder.

'Shit, is there no escape?'

'Relax,' she said, 'I was kidding. It's only Petri.' Ash turned to see Barry Petri approaching.

'I don't know how you can sit here, it reeks, and look at that tasteful bucket of fag-ends,' he said.

'We come here because there's less chance of bumping into you,' said Ali. He made a face and pulled up a chair.

'Are you eating?' he asked.

'I'm getting my calories from the champagne,' Ali said.

'In the middle of the day too,' said Barry Petri. 'Is it really champagne ...? Are we celebrating something?'

'No we are not and if we were you can be sure you wouldn't be invited.'

'Please children,' Ash said, 'you're making my head ache.'

He'd worked with Ali for a long time. Her sharp tongue could still take him by surprise but she was a brilliant clinician and the patients loved her.

'... he's ready for something else,' Ali was saying. 'He's done well ... Perhaps you could take him into your new group, Ash?'

'Who?' Ash asked.

'My lonesome lad,' she said.

'I thought he was your favourite,' said Petri.

'I don't have favourites,' snapped Ali. 'What about it Ash? Any chance?' Before he could answer, she said, 'I'll get Rosemary to make an appointment.' Then she said 'You can at least see him. I think he'd do well.' Barry was tucking into the plate of pasta that had arrived.

'You'll get fat,' said Ali. 'And you'll get liver cancer,' said Barry. Ash drained his mineral water.

'Bye you two,' he said. 'I need some air.'

'Hey Ash ... I'll catch you later. I'll send up the notes.'

Ali inhaled and blew the smoke towards Barry. She hadn't planned to sit here with him. He was staring at her. He smiled suddenly and in that split second she knew that he was going to say something personal.

'Ali ...' Only her close friends called her that. 'Ali ...' he tried again, 'there is something I wanted to ask you.'

'Look at the time. Sorry Barry – I'm out of here. Enjoy the pasta.'

Swinging expertly out of the bench seat she was across the patio and out without a backward glance. She walked rapidly towards the car park. She still wanted a drink. She crossed the road and went into Strakers. Not her favourite but she wouldn't be here long. A quick glance told her that there was no one she recognised here. She ordered a double gin and tonic followed fairly rapidly by another. Even before the man at the bar had started to move in her direction she was outside again.

She drove back to the clinic, sending up a spatter of gravel as she parked. She heard the car door slam though didn't think she'd slammed it. Brenda was on reception. She turned to the stairs looking carefully at the first step. She didn't want to fall flat on her face in front of brittle Brenda.

She went to her desk and opening the drawer searched for the tin of 'Fisherman's Friend'. There was a knock on the door.

'Come ... in.' She shoved the drawer shut. Brenda appeared in the doorway.

'Dr Slade.'

'What?'

'There was a message for you.'

'So – write it down. Put it in my tray.'

'But he said ...'

'Said what?'

'That he ...'

'For Christ sake Brenda. Just take a message. I was at lunch.' The door shut. Ali was across the room and yanking the door open.

'Brenda …' Brenda was disappearing down the stairs. 'Brenda. Brenda …'

'What?' said Brenda, facing her.

'Don't go off like that. I was talking to you.'

'And I was talking to you,' Brenda said. She continued down the stairs.

'Write it down and put it in my tray,' Ali shouted. She turned and walked back to her room. She felt a bit sick. She wasn't used to people talking to her like that. Little bitch.

The afternoon stretched ahead. She opened her diary. Her head hurt. Three appointments. She looked at the clock. Two o'clock. Then what? Home. Television. Bottle of wine. Her mouth felt sour. She rummaged around and found the 'Fisherman's Friend'. Perhaps she and Ash could go for a drink at the weekend. Bugger. She'd said she would visit her dad this weekend. She got up and walked to the window. Brent was digging one of the flowerbeds. He looked so absorbed. It must be good to be so engaged in something so … real. Must help with the drink. Take your mind off it. Sighing she picked up the pile of papers.

She returned to her desk. She needed to buy some whiskey to take and she was out of gin. If she went to the supermarket she'd have to go into town. She'd go to the corner shop … again. She'd already been in twice this week for booze. Old Patel was OK, she could have a laugh with him but she didn't like his mother. She sniffed disapproval. 'Well – sod her,' she said out loud and kicked the drawer shut with her foot. Sod them all. She got up and strode to the door. She glanced in the propped mirror and saw a striking figure in chiselled stilettos and black suit, imperious, invincible. No outward sign of the ever-present emptiness that only the drink numbed.

At the bottom of the stairs she glanced to the left. Brenda was leaning against the group room door.

'What are you doing?' Brenda saw her and jumped away from the door. 'I asked what were you doing?'

'Nothing. I thought I heard shouting. I wanted to see if he was all right.'

'Who?'

'Dr Jones.'

'Brenda – you were listening.'

'I told you I thought I heard shouting.' Brenda walked past her into the office and shut the door. Ali opened the door and followed her in.

'Brenda. I'm fed up with your attitude. You were listening and you know it. What were you listening for?'

'Nothing … I wanted to see if he was all right. Brian was really angry this morning. He carries a knife you know.'

'Is it your job to look after him?'

'No – but he's on his own in there. I just wanted to see – it doesn't matter.'

'Brenda … you know I should report you.'

'Yea – and I should report you.'

'Report me – what for?'

'You know.' She didn't but she felt herself reddening. The door opened and Rosemary came in.

'Hello Dr Slade. Can I help?'

'No,' said Ali. 'It's … nothing.'

She left the room and walked back upstairs. She felt shaky and unnerved. What had she meant? What could she know? There was nothing in her work to question. What could she have been referring to? She wanted that woman out. In her office, she reached to the back of the drawer. Her fingers found the bottle. Glancing at the door, she unscrewed the top and took a long swig. She wiped her mouth, screwed the top back on and pushed the bottle to the back of the drawer.

Chapter 8
Renée

Ash pressed his fingers together in a familiar gesture. 'My dreams are bizarre ... I wake up exhausted.' The fan hummed quietly. Ash sat opposite her, cradled in the blue armchair. Today he looked troubled, his shoulders low. 'Do you think it can get to us in the end?' he said. 'I sometimes wonder ... like nurses ... all that blood and gore ... is that why they need to party and be wild, to forget?'

Renée waited knowing that he didn't expect an answer. 'What is it,' she said, 'has something happened?'

'Not really.' He shifted in the chair. 'No, nothing new has happened. Well, no more than usual. Maybe I'm just tired.' He looked at the floor. 'I find myself wondering if anybody is really happy.'

'Are you?' she asked. He smiled.

'Yes, well ... you know.' He had a good smile. 'I'm worried that I'm getting in touch with madness again. I thought I was over all that.'

'Since when have you been afraid of madness?'

'Other people's I don't mind, but not my own ...' He stared into the corner of the room. She had seen that look once before.

'Is there something in particular that you're worried about?'

'No. Well, I suppose there is but it's something and nothing.' He sat forward. 'Last week Petri asked me to assess a woman who works at the centre with the idea that she might join a group.'

'At 'The Firs'?'

'No, no. She'd have to go to Fairfield's, if she agreed to therapy. But that's not really the point. The point is that I was in a hurry and I think I wasn't clear about it not being for my group. It shouldn't be a problem. Barry will sort it out, but it's left me rattled and I don't know why.'

'It sounds like Barry's problem. Why doesn't he assess her? Why is she being assessed anyway?'

'It's a bit complicated and ... it involves Ali.' Renée drew in a breath.

'How?'

'I'm not quite sure. I gather Barry is afraid that this woman is going to put in a complaint about her.' Renée straightened in the chair.

'What is the complaint about?' She said, aware of some irritation at the mention of Ali Slade.

'I don't know. You know Ali. She's brilliant, but she can be difficult. I don't know the details.' Renée kept her face impassive. 'Barry seems reluctant to talk about it and I don't really want to get involved. But, the thing is, any dealings I have with this new woman leave me unsettled and doubting my competence and I don't know why she has this effect.' Renée glanced at the clock. The session had already run over by two minutes and they would have to finish. For now, she thought, she would put her irritation down to some maternal concern for Ash and her feeling that any contact with Ali was not in his best interest.

'We need to finish,' she said. 'See how it goes this week and I'll see you next Tuesday.'

Ash walked over to the hat stand and put on his coat.

'How's Tom doing?' she asked. He stood for a moment.

'OK. You know. It isn't easy but thanks for asking. Perhaps when we've got a bit more time?' Renée nodded.

'Of course.' He walked to the door and shut it quietly behind him.

Renée sat for a moment. The room was full of feeling. It was getting dark outside, but she didn't want to put on the light. Arnold would have started the supper. The house would be warm and both of them would be pleased that she was home.

Still she sat. Ash had taken something with him when he left. She wondered whether she would discuss any of this with Arnold. Somehow she thought she wouldn't. Was Ash lonely? He seemed to like his present life but she wished he could find someone to share more of it. She half wished she'd invited him for Shabbat but she sensed that at the moment he wanted to be on his own. She got up from the chair, resisting the wish to remain seated in the darkening room reflecting on, she almost didn't know what ... passage of time perhaps. She tidied up the few papers, locked the filing cabinet and taking her coat from the stand, shrugged herself into it, pulled the thick woolly collar up around her neck. She was becoming sentimental, she thought.

Renée peeled the skin from the second onion and chopped it into chunky pieces. She scraped them into the pan. The smell of fresh frying onions and herbs matched the comfortable kitchen. She pulled a chair over and began to trim the leeks. She worked automatically, her mind going over the day. She could hear Arnold in the dining room preparing the table. Arnold liked to keep to tradition and she too liked Shabbat and it meant they saw the children and grandchildren once a week.

Her legs felt tired. Getting older had made her heavier. She didn't like it but it didn't preoccupy her and she was not prepared to diet. 'Mine little dumpling' Arnold would say, pinching her waist knowing how it irritated her but enjoying the reaction. She'd been a pretty young woman but she was comfortable with the transition of the no longer pretty but pleasant face she saw in the mirror. Her blue eyes were still bright and her expression, she imagined, was kindly.

Through the hatch Arnold's shadow moved back and forth. She heard him grunt as he stretched up to take the menorah from the top cupboard. She heard the sideboard door squeak and heard him rummaging for the matches. Any minute now he would come into the kitchen, asking where the matches were. He appeared in the doorway.

'*Liebling* – where have you put the matches?'

'I haven't put them anywhere, but maybe you put them with the tallit in the drawer.' They exchanged a smile born of years and she knew that, under the irritation, it was moments like this that bound them together. She heard his flat-footed tread as he returned to the other room and moments later, the rattle of the matches as he shook the box.

She had not expected to have such a happy life. Life has not always been easy for them. She loved her children and adored her grandchildren. Mark was intelligent and funny and Shonah was beautiful and happily married with two wonderful children. If she thought of her mother's life, she felt blessed. She gathered the vegetable peelings into the centre of the spread newspaper and folded it into a parcel ready to go to the compost.

She stood up, wiping her hand on her apron. A clatter of cutlery came from the dining room. She sighed. She fetched plates from the cupboard, counted them and put them on the sideboard. She opened the fridge and took out a plate of gefilte fish. There would have been enough for Ash. It was good that they had arranged to meet next week. In some ways he was so self-sufficient and it was hard for him to ask for what he needed. She took off her apron. Through the hatch she heard Arnold begin humming *Hava Nagila* and knew, without looking, that he would be polishing the cutlery.

Chapter 9

She had been listening, of course. Dr Slade was right. She might report her but so what? She still had the whip hand. Dr Slade's breath confirmed that. Eleven o'clock and the gin was already on her breath.

Brenda went into the group room on the pretence of tidying up. There was a small glass vase with flowers on the table. Had he arranged them? No, men don't do flowers. Anyway she would have seen him. Somehow though, she knew he had. Chosen them from a garden – his garden? Selected the colours. Cut the stems. Bleeding hearts, a red tulip, a peachy rose and in the middle a white nettle. Did he live in the country then? Somewhere near hedgerows?

Someone had opened the window. Where did he sit? Which was his chair? Probably this one, so he could see the door. See them as they came in. She lowered herself onto the chair. It was warm. She breathed in. There was a curious smell. Dusty, warm. Was there a hint of him? But all those other smells would be here too. All those others sharing him, receiving his glances, eating his words.

She stood up abruptly. Plants needed watering. On the side table there was the usual clutter: paper, felt tip pens, a paperclip. Under one chair was a pen. Not the usual sort. Had it dropped out of his pocket? The pocket of his linen jacket. The top pocket. The one nearest to his heart. She banged a pile of leaflets into neatness. She could think it was his. Have a reason to return it to him. 'Did you drop your pen Dr Jones? I found it in the group room.'

She thought she smelt dog. Did he have a dog? A dog that padded beside him, tail wagging as they walked along a country lane. He would like the country, she decided. He would know different trees and the names of flowers. He would pick blackberries in late summer to take home to …. She fetched a glass of water from the kitchen and watered each plant in turn. She broke off the dry brown leaves and turned each pot round to the light. She sniffed her fingers. The acidy smell of the African violet was on her fingers. He might notice she'd cared for the plants. Think her considerate. It would be an unspoken communication between them. Both of them taking care of the environment.

The upstairs room was empty. She knew Dr Slade was with a patient. She let the door close behind her. His jacket was on the back of the chair. Blue and white striped seersucker. She'd noticed it this morning. She crossed the room to his desk. The jacket was not on the chair back properly. She straightened it. Slowly she traced round the collar. Running her hands down the jacket side, she slipped her hand into the pocket. There was a button in the corner. She retrieved her hand. Again she smoothed her hand down the jacket and into the other pocket. A handkerchief. The neat folds tamed her slight recoil. She glanced at the door and bending down, she breathed in the garment's signature. Slightly minty. Some sort of aftershave – musky. A metallic smell.

She heard a step. She moved rapidly towards the filing cabinet. The door opened. Dr Jones appeared.

'Brenda …?' he said. 'Can I help?'

'Files,' she said. 'They need filing. Dr Slade asked me.' She moved towards the door. The pen was warm in her hand. 'Dr Jones. I found this pen. I thought it might be yours.' He took the pen almost touching her fingers. He looked at it quickly and then held it out to her.

'It isn't mine, thank you,' he said. He smiled and held the door open for her. In the corridor she stood for a minute. It was too quick. She took the pen and pressed it lightly against her cheek. He had said thank you and smiled but she had expected more. Perhaps he didn't want to show that he was pleased that she had come all the way upstairs to bring the pen to him. She looked at it again. Well, it was hers now. Quite a nice pen actually.

Chapter 10
Leila

Leila sat in her new blue Astra and wishing that she hadn't arrived quite so early. The car park was empty except for a black convertible parked in one of the designated spaces, and an immaculate silver Jag. A notice indicated further parking round the back. Near the door a bicycle with a wicker basket was padlocked to a metal post.

The house was set back from the road with stone pillars on either side of the entrance. A board, badly needing painting, displayed the name 'The Firs'. She counted the windows. Three on either side of the door and on two storeys. Around the car park there were borders with shrubs, the ubiquitous sort that surround communal buildings: plants suitable for annexes, schools, hospitals – minimum care needed. These had dull yellow flowers or white berries. At least there were no crisp packets or rubbish impaled on the spikes. In the corner, a tree covered in ivy was pushing up the tarmac. She stepped out of the car and shut the door carefully. This was her first visit and she was surprisingly nervous.

She walked towards the entrance as a car turned into the drive. It was a green Morris Minor with worn woodwork and she caught a glimpse of a man with a lot of wavy hair. Near the door there was a flowerpot spilling over with cigarette ends.

She pushed open the glass door. On a bench just inside there was a comic with a torn cover and three umbrellas in a blue jar. A red umbrella, with its spines twisted, lay beside it and a single coat hung on a peg. She pushed open the second door. There was a reception desk but nobody there. A vase of faded anemones and a blue book marked 'Visitors' was on the desk. Leila took in the familiar smell, a mixture of polish, disinfectant, smoke and something indistinguishable. She stood for a moment. The sound of a mop clanking against a bucket came from an open door to the left. Perhaps that was the owner of the bicycle? A door opened and a woman came out of the office behind the desk. She had glasses and a straight greyish bob held back with an Alice band. She smiled pleasantly.

'Can I help you?' she asked.

'I'm Leila Scott. I'm here to see Dr Jones.' The woman nodded.

'You're the new student. Fine. He's expecting you. I think he's in.' She craned forward to look through the door into the car park. 'Yes, his car's there. He'll be upstairs. I'll just call him and tell him you're here.' She picked up the phone. 'Dr Jones … Leila Scott is here to see you. Shall I send her up?' She put the phone down.

'If you go to the top of the stairs and turn left, you'll find his room, second one along. It's called 'Cedar'. You can't miss it.' She smiled again, an interested, questioning smile, as if she would have liked to know more. Leila thanked her and walked to the stairs.

As she walked up the stairs she remembered last week's interview with the tall and imperious Gabriella Clayburgh, consultant psychiatrist. Why did she want to work with groups, she'd asked? What advantages did she think groups had over individual work? How did she expect to get her referrals? How would she tell who was suitable? Dr Jones would be running the group but she shouldn't expect to be spoon-fed. What was her particular interest? Leila felt she failed on all counts. She hoped she would not have to go through it all again with Dr Jones.

She found the door marked 'Cedar' and knocked gently. Nothing happened. She knocked again, a bit harder.

'Come in,' a voice called. A man in a blue shirt was sitting at the far desk. He wore a navy-blue sleeveless jumper. He replaced the receiver and swivelled to face her.

'Hello, you must be Leila?' He got up and extended his hand. He was about fifty, she thought.

'Good to meet you Leila.' He indicated a chair. 'Have a seat.' He sat back down.

'You found it all right … well … obviously. So – this is your second placement. Where did you do your first one?

He asked her a lot of questions, she thought afterwards, but in a gentle way. She told him a lot too. She was surprised. Surprised that she told him she was nervous. That she found beginning difficult, that her first group had almost closed because of lack of referrals. All this he listened to, sometimes with his hands behind his head, sometimes watching her in an interested way. She relaxed. At one point, a slight, nervy man rushed in. Dr Jones introduced him as Dr Petri. He gave her a distracted smile and shook her hand briefly. He had rather nice grey leather shoes, she noticed.

Dr Jones' group met on a Thursday at ten o'clock. It would be helpful if she could get here a bit earlier in case there were any messages or something needed passing on. If the group members arrived early they could make a coffee or go into the group room, which would be open ten minutes before the group started. She and Dr Jones would not go in until ten o'clock. He looked forward to working with her and if she didn't mind, he would like her to meet the group before she looked at any notes. Was that all right with her? That way it allowed her to value her first impressions without too much prior knowledge, or prejudice, he added with a smile. He would see her on Thursday. Before she knew it she was out of the door.

She walked thoughtfully to the stairs. A youngish man was starting up the stairs.

'No, you first. Not that I'm superstitious but ...' he smiled. Leila recognised the man from the Morris Minor.

The woman with the Alice band was behind the desk.

'All right?' she said. 'Would you like a coffee? The kitchen is down there on the left. Help yourself. When you're here all the time there's a saucer for the money. I'm Rosemary, by the way. Nice to meet you.'

Back in the warmth of her car, Leila sat for a minute. Another hurdle over. She'd met Dr Jones and he seemed OK. There was still the group to negotiate but she wouldn't be on her own. She felt a flutter of excitement.

Chapter 11
Ali

The door burst open.

'Ash!' Ali demanded, 'What's this about Brenda Chit? She's been asked to leave. Did you know?' Ash sighed and put down his pen. 'She's really overstepped the mark this time. Had some sort of screaming match with Rosemary in front of the patients. Good.'

'Oh Come on Ali.'

'Oh, I know. But you know what I mean. The woman's nothing but trouble. She's so above herself. How are you anyway? I called you at the weekend. You're hiding yourself away again.'

She perched on the edge of his desk. There was something about his desk that attracted sitting on. He took off his glasses and leaned back in his chair. Ali's long legs extended towards him. Shiny stockings and pointed black ankle boots extended from a short black skirt. On her jacket she had a large brooch made out of watch parts. The light reflected on her sleek black bob, and dark eyes looked at him from under her geometric fringe. She really was extremely attractive.

'Are you up for a drink tonight?' Ash hesitated. She slid off the desk. 'I'll catch you later.' Ash returned to his file. At the door Ali turned.

'You know she had a thing about you, don't you?' She smiled and was gone.

Ash frowned. He assumed she was talking about Brenda but he didn't know what she meant. No doubt she would explain later. It was strange though how much interest was generated around Brenda. He shrugged and returned to the notes.

Chapter 12
9.55 Thursday

Starting a new group always made Ash anxious. He was pleased to have Leila in the group this year. Her presence might bring some stability and he liked her straightforwardness. He hoped all the group members would turn up. That always helped.

It was a cold day. Leaves cascaded from the trees and the autumn colours delighted him as usual. In the garden Brent raked the leaves into heaps, working tirelessly against the wind, which periodically tossed the neat piles into untidiness again. Patiently, he gathered them together once more, lifting them into the wheelbarrow and carting them to a place hidden behind the oak tree. Ash watched him for several minutes, Brent's methodical care giving him a sense of peace and order. He turned back from the window as Leila came into the room. She looked as if she'd brushed her hair and put on lipstick. He nodded at the clock and smiled.

'Ready?' he asked.

'Ready,' she said, and they left the room together.

Chapter 13
Steph

'Can I ask you something?' Elaine put down the tray and half turned. Steph's heart quickened. The tea steamed on the tray. If she came out and asked her, Elaine might smile, take the tea into the office and then come back ready to talk. Or, she might look embarrassed, mutter something and afterwards avoid her. Later, seeing Elaine with the others, looking her way, she would imagine they were discussing her, saying how sad she was. The tea was developing a thin sheen. She'd always thought Elaine so attractive but close to she was rather puffy. Elaine's smile was becoming a little fixed.

'What did you want to ask?' Elaine said at last.

'Oh nothing … it can wait … tea's getting cold. I'll catch you some other time.' Clearly relieved, Elaine picked up the tray and walked towards the office.

Dr Jones had said that he didn't expect group members to meet outside of the weekly sessions. She'd felt really disappointed when he said that. That was one of her reasons for joining the group, to meet people. There was bound to be somebody she liked, but then he said they weren't to meet outside. What was the point of that? She'd been told that joining a group might help her feel more comfortable with people but if she couldn't meet up with them, how was that supposed to work?

On the bus she sat near the back and put her bag on the seat next to her. The driver greeted everybody as they came on the bus. Most looked surprised, but then smiled at his friendliness. Before the bus was half full, she found it irritating. The windows were steamy and she rubbed a circle with her finger. Immediately she heard her mother's voice.

'Leave that window alone. It'll make a mark.' She looked to see if anybody had noticed. The man opposite was reading a paper and the woman with the child was bending over talking to her. Nobody was watching her. Who would? she thought. Who would be watching her anyway?

They were passing the wooded bit before descending into the town. People in bright anoraks and boots walked along the path and a man stood balancing against a car putting on his boots. Friends, couples. Everybody had someone to be with, she thought, remembering Elaine and how nearly she'd humiliated herself by asking her. Of course she wouldn't have wanted to go for a drink with her. The bus stopped and an old lady walked slowly to the door. Why didn't the silly cow sit nearer the front? More people got on and the bus moved off.

Look at that lot there, walking in pairs and chatting. How did they do that? Did one of them say 'why don't we go for a walk on Saturday' and they all said 'oh yes, let's' and then they were in the pub having a nice time, drinking and chatting.

Were they happy, really? Did that man really want to be with that woman, or was he wishing he was somewhere else, with someone else? Would they still be out walking in a year's time? No, probably he would be bored to death with her and eyeing up the other women. Stop it! She only imagined they weren't happy so she wouldn't feel so bad, but it didn't work. She wanted a friend to walk with, a friend to have a drink with, a friend who would tolerate her. She could be a good friend, couldn't she?

The bus descended into town. It was quite crowded. In the high street she saw couples, friends, talking, laughing, looking in windows. Clutching arms as they crossed the road, holding hands, couples, friends, people, with each other, getting on with things. She looked at her watch. It was nine-thirty. It would take ten minutes to walk to 'The Firs'. She was in good time.

She pulled her bag closer, hugging it to her. She would be a good friend, if anybody wanted her, if anybody knew. She could put a notice on her forehead; stick a notice up at work. *Not* wanted a room to rent, drop leaf table to sell, just wanted a friend, nothing heavy. Someone to do things with, to want to be with her, sometimes.

The bus stopped. She waited for the other passengers to leave their seats. Some thanked the driver. As she reached him he smiled.

'Have a nice day,' he said.

'You too,' she said quickly, but faintly audible as she stepped down she muttered 'arsehole'.

Chapter 14

Norma

Norma opened her eyes a minute before the alarm. She turned it off and folded the sheet back neatly. She got out of bed and put on her slippers.

In the bathroom she ran a modest amount of water into the sink and washed in a methodical and functional manner, only once glancing into the slightly steamed up mirror. She emptied the water and, reaching for the cloth, wiped round the sink and under the soap. She folded the cloth neatly and put it back on the pipe and put on her dressing gown over her winceyette nightdress. The bedroom was colder than the bathroom but she simply noted these minor discomforts and the electric fire remained off. She frowned slightly as she recalled her bad dream.

She stepped out into the street. It was a cold day. Her plain calf-length mac was not really a sensible garment for this weather and she congratulated herself for her continued wearing of a vest. A man was walking towards her. She dropped her gaze, resisting the urge to tuck her hands into her sleeves.

The bus was full and she found a seat at the back. For the first time she allowed herself to think about the day ahead. On days like today she wondered at the sense of what she had given up, in order to do, what? To be in the real world. To live. To spend from eight thirty to five o'clock doing work that was trivial in the extreme and, dare she say it, boring. But these thoughts were unproductive. The work was important to somebody, her boss anyway, it seemed. Who was she to question and have such self-centred thoughts? And this morning she had the group and the morning off.

She'd been surprised when her boss had so readily agreed to the weekly commitment. It seems she was 'worth her weight in gold' and if she was really worried, she could make up the time when they were busy. She wondered why she had worried so much, but then she was still surprised at the values of the ordinary world. Nobody else wanted the early stop. She pressed the bell.

Her small watch told her it was nine forty. It was just a short walk from here, so she wouldn't be late. She pushed down the wave of anxiety, employing a technique she'd developed over years. She thought about her blessings and told herself that she had enough food, her clothes were warm and that she should be grateful.

This was a part of town she didn't know well and she felt the familiar separateness from the people she passed, imagining they saw a tall thin woman, glancing in the shop windows. Suddenly she was struck by the display in a window, the wood surround an unusual shade of green. She saw wisps of lace and delicate flowers on tiny bras and knickers. She wanted to turn away but she was drawn to the pretty feminine garments. She had only just relinquished the thick brassieres she'd worn for years, designed to flatten and hide. She felt a thrill as she looked at these beautiful creations. She shouldn't be looking. She walked on looking in other windows, bemused by the colourful fashions and wondering how people knew what to choose. Could she? Wasn't she a woman too? What would it feel like to wear underwear like that? But even as she thought it, she knew she could never enter one of these shops with their bright displays and confident music. A clock on the wall by the newsagents told her that it was nine forty-five.

Chapter 15
First session

Two people were in the group room when Ash and Leila arrived. Norma and the man Ronnie, who looked up and nodded to Ash. Ash took a seat facing the door and Leila sat opposite him, next to Norma and with an empty seat on the other side. Norma smiled at Leila. Ash hoped that the person he'd heard in the kitchen was one of the group and realised that he was more anxious about so few group members being here because of Leila. On his own he would have simply noticed it and thought about what it might mean.

Steph was the next to arrive. She looked surly, glanced sharply at him and closed the door behind her. He was about to ask her to leave it open but hesitated. He didn't want to make her feel she had done something wrong. Steph walked over to a pile of chairs, put her coat on them and stood looking at the circle. Ash wondered which seat she would choose as there was no chair without at least one person next to it. She stood, uncertain, then took the seat two chairs away from him and next to Norma. Norma glanced at her, gave a smile but Steph didn't look at her. She pushed her bag under her chair.

The door handle rattled. They all looked up. A moment later the handle rattled again and Carl, looking taller than Ash remembered, put his head round the door. Behind him was Linda.

'You can leave it open,' Ash said. The man opened the door wide.

'We weren't sure which room it was,' Carl said. He crossed the room quickly and took the seat next but one to Ash. Ash was glad to see Linda who'd phoned in the week, full of anxiety about the first session. Linda looked round then walked to the piled up chairs and began to unwind a long scarf. She smiled nervously at him and took the chair next to Steph. Steph visibly shrank. Interesting, thought Ash, that the one person who hated people close to her, was the one they sat by.

Ash welcomed them and the group fell silent, several looking to him to give them a lead. Leila too, looked anxiously at him. After a few minutes, Norma introduced herself and suggested that it might be a good idea if they all gave their names. Ronnie nodded and gave his name. Linda said her name and looked down. Her hair was brushed forward covering her hearing aid. Nobody else volunteered their name and nobody else asked. Norma asked if anybody else was as nervous as she was. Steph asked what they were supposed to be doing.

'Getting to know each other?' volunteered Norma. Steph gave her a withering look. Ash wondered how robust Norma was and whether she would be able to stand up to Steph. He might have to help her a little, but for today, he would see how they got on.

They had all turned up except April Rose and the man Barry had referred. April, he was not surprised about, but he was irritated by the man he'd been persuaded to take on not turning up. Now there were two empty chairs and even if the man never appeared, he was in a sense already here and it would have to be dealt with.

Chapter 16
Peter

Peter, the man in question, was on platform six waiting for a Circle Line train. He knew now that he might be late. His brother had promised to get him to the station in time but he couldn't wake him so he'd had to run to the station. The carpet in the living room was dirty and the sleeping bag he'd been given smelled of urine. A forty watt bulb in the bathroom showed that the bathroom too was filthy. He'd splashed water on his face and dried it on the corner of a thin towel hanging behind the door and cleaned his teeth with his finger and a bit of toothpaste squeezed out of a nearly empty tube.

There was nothing in the kitchen except some tea bags and two slices of bread in the bottom of the packet. The pizza boxes from last night and one dried up slice sprawled across the table. The fridge had mould and there was no milk. Maybe he could get something on the train. It was so different without Mum here and he was pleased to be leaving. At that moment he didn't ever want to see his brother again.

He hated rushing. His Paddington train was at eight o'clock and unless the tube came soon he would miss it. He couldn't bear to arrive late. He shouldn't have stayed over. The tannoy announced that the train was expected either in two or ten minutes. Peter wasn't sure which. The platform was filling up. People stood really near the edge, two and three deep. When the train came he would be squashed up against other people. His breathing got faster. He looked at his watch again. If the train came soon he might still make the connection.

'The train approaching platform six is a Circle Line train via Euston Square.' As the train slowed into the station he saw that each carriage that passed was fuller than the one before. Opposite him the doors opened. Three people got out. People moved forward. He put his foot into the carriage. There wasn't room. Tentatively he pushed the back in front of him. It shuffled forward slightly.

'Mind the doors'. In panic Peter pushed. The man moved forward and the door closed behind him catching his hair. His face was close up against the jacket of the man in front. He was wedged, unable to move, nothing to hold on to, unable to work out how he would get out if the platform at his station was on the opposite side.

There were five minutes left of the session. Ash found himself focussing on the empty chairs. It seemed easier to think about who wasn't here rather than who was. Linda had asked why the chairs were there. A sharp look at Leila stopped her answering the question immediately. Linda said, maybe they were too frightened.

'Like you were?' Ash said. Norma said perhaps they were stuck in the traffic or had missed the bus. Nobody responded. Steph asked why he couldn't tell them. Didn't he know?

'I don't see why you can't answer,' she persisted. 'Is this what it is going to be like?'

'Perhaps we're not meant to know, or ask.' Norma said. Steph looked at her. Norma looked down. Ash said that it seemed difficult not knowing who the chairs were for and whether they were going to join the group. Steph snorted.

'Stating the bleeding obvious,' she muttered. There was a knock on the door and a smallish man put his head round the door.

'Sorry I'm late.' He looked imploringly at Ash, who nodded and smiled.

'Come in,' Ash said. Peter smiled gratefully, walked over and took the seat next to him. He sat perched on the edge of the chair, smiling and nodding at everybody. His face was red and damp strands of hair stuck to the back of his neck.

'I'm sorry I'm late,' he began again. 'I missed my train connection. I had to take the next one and change. I'm sorry. I'm Peter by the way.'

'I'm Norma,' said Norma. 'I'm glad you've made it.' She trailed off, perhaps wondering if she'd said too much. Peter relaxed and sat back in his chair. Ash looked round. He sensed that the group were relieved at Peter's arrival. He glanced at Leila, who smiled.

It was the end of the session. The group, after the uncomfortable start felt more settled.

'It's time to finish,' Ash said. 'I will see you next week.' They looked surprised. Steph looking annoyed, got up quickly, picked up her coat and left the room. Peter got up and looked at Ash as if expecting him to say something.

'Is it next week – the same?' He looked at Leila, who nodded and smiled. He again apologised to Ash for being late, said that he would be on time next week and left the room.

There was nobody in the kitchen as Ash and Leila walked by. He heard the toilet flush as they passed and on the landing he looked out and saw Norma crossing the car park and Ronnie, leaning against the tree, smoking.

Chapter 17

When she'd dealt with the cloud's post, Jessica left the office and walked along the corridor to Drew's room. He was sitting at his desk.
'You OK?'
'What do you think? I know I've blown it.' Jessica put a hand on his shoulder. 'I knew it as soon as I started. All morning I'd been sorting stuff for this returnic and every time his anger came up, it triggered something but I kept pushing it away. I was so in denial that it was still a problem for me then I let rip at Julius – gentle conscientious Julius. He'd done nothing wrong, he didn't deserve it. And look, he held up a piece of glass, 'I've broken my paperweight. So I'll be going back down again too, who knows for how long or what they'll set up for me.'
'I am sorry,' said Jessica. 'I wish I could have done something.'
'Shall we walk?' said Drew standing up suddenly.
The meadow was white with poppies and peonies; snowdrops and white lavender scented the air. Knowing that she was leaving added to its beauty. It would be good to lie down in the soft grassland, close her eyes and dream herself into forgetfulness.
Drew stopped. 'Look there's no one waiting at the cliff.' Ahead the meadow came to an abrupt end. 'Why don't we go and look? Since we're both returning, we could at least have a look at where we are going and I can see how my morning planning has worked out. Shall we take a look?
From the platform, as the mist parted, a landscape opened out below them. The first thing that struck her was the colour. Although muted it seemed sharp against her unpractised eye. She saw green fields, roads and box-like houses, seas and rivers. Filaments of clouds drifted across their view. Now she saw a building. There were figures but too far away to see any detail.
'It's so different,' she said. 'It's cramped. I don't understand it. I don't recognise anything and I don't understand it. Is that my return?'

'I think it must be.' Even as they watched the picture faded. *'A glimpse,'* he said, *'they've given us a glimpse.'*

Chapter 18
Just an ordinary day…

Brenda woke at five thirty on that morning of November the third. It was still dark outside. She got out of bed, walked to the window, drew back one curtain and went into the bathroom. The light above the wall cabinet threw her face into focus. The same dull, sallow face. She stepped on the scales. She hadn't put on any weight. She showered and dressed in her housework clothes.

She made a pot of tea and as she sat sipping it, she tried to throw off last night's dream. It was the familiar theme where she was struggling and out of control. She took her cup into the kitchen, deciding that she would wash the floor and hoover through. In the bedroom, she tidied everything away and stripping the bed, made it from the beginning, smoothing the sheets and the bedcover so that not a crease could be seen.

By six thirty she had cleaned every surface and wiped round the bathroom. She had fifteen minutes for breakfast. She turned on the television for the news and to see what was on that evening. Just like last night she would be here, on her own, watching crappy television and hating her life. She poured some cereal into a bowl and made another pot of tea. Then, having washed up and wiped the surfaces once more, she dressed in the blouse she had ironed last night and combed her hair back from her face. At eight thirty she left for work. Just another ordinary day, but it wasn't.

Chapter 19
The ward

The ward round was at ten thirty. Brenda had been up since six. The day room was empty and only the night nurses were around and they were in the office chatting and didn't bother her. She'd cleaned her room and made her bed. She thought the day room dirty and the cleaners lazy but she couldn't say anything. They only hoovered round the sofas, collected the dirty cups and took them to the kitchen and they didn't clean the surfaces and hadn't mopped the floor since she'd been here. She would have liked to clean it properly; she knew where they kept the cleaning stuff, but then they would say she was obsessive and she didn't want to give them any more ammunition.

At seven thirty she made some toast and went back into the day room. Tony was in there now, hugging a cushion and rocking and making that horrible noise in his throat. How could they think she should be here with people like him? Chrissie had been round to check she'd had her medication. Some of the others began wandering in, not even dressed, walking around in slippers like it was home. Chrissie had asked if she was all right. How could she be all right in here? she'd wanted to retort but she just said, yes she was fine.

The room was filling up and the woman with the dyed black hair who shouted, came in with a mug of something. Raja was sitting in the corner curled up in the chair. She had a red spot on her forehead this morning.

She would go to her room in a minute. She didn't want to be on her own but she didn't want to be in here either where somebody might come up to her and ask her why she was here and what had she done. It was none of their fucking business and she shouldn't be here anyway.

In the kitchen she washed up her plate and cup, dried them and put them away in the cupboard. The shelf was dirty. She put her cup the right way up and pushed it to the back so she could find it again. There was a broken yellow cup handle with a jagged edge. She put it at the back, near the mug. She went back to her room and listened to the news on her small radio.

She liked political programmes but wondered how people knew so much. Even Tony with his rocking, seemed to know who people were and which parties they represented. It made her feel ignorant. There'd just never been anyone to talk to about things like that. She could talk to her Mum, but she didn't know anything about politics and stuff, and anyway, she died. Dad was just ignorant, and a bully. She hoped she wasn't like him.

The news had a sort of lulling effect. She listened to it when she felt lonely. Sometimes she listened to the parliamentary reports.

Last year she bought a book in a remainder bookshop, *A Short History of the World*. It was interesting but it left even more questions and there was nobody to ask. Better to say nothing and only talk about what she needed to. It was only at work she talked anyway. People like Rosemary seemed quite happy to chat about total bollocks as far as she was concerned. Sometimes she wanted to scream with boredom. Didn't they know there was a world out there? And, most of them had been to decent schools. Rosemary's parents were teachers and they'd educated her and her sister at home, so they must have known a thing or two. Privy Comprehensive was not exactly a seat of learning and anyway, she'd left just when it was getting interesting.

'Why don't you go to evening classes?' Rosemary had said, one day when she had been saying something about the last war.

'Do you know then?' she'd wanted to retort, 'Do you know when the Yalta Conference was?' But she didn't, afraid that Rosemary would know. Anyway, what good did it do to know? It only left more things she didn't know.

There was more activity outside. Chrissie popped her head round to see if she was all right. What did she think; she'd try to top herself again? No chance here; there was the odd blunt kitchen knife. She could shred her sheets for a noose of course, but she'd have to hide it all between the 'just popping their heads round'. She felt empty and stuck. Chrissie left her door open. They preferred it like that. 'Makes you less isolated,' she'd said. 'You might want to talk to somebody or why not sit in the day room?' What with them? The new man, Bass, was all right except he thought himself superior. He had jet black hair.

She wondered if he dyed it. His son visited him every Tuesday and Thursday.

What would it be like to have a father who taught you things? Practical things like how to mend a puncture or fix things on your car, and what if he could teach you things like history and literature? Someone like … Dr Jones. She pictured him, in his blue shirt, reading in a comfy chair. Imagine having him as a father. She thought he had children. Somebody had said something once. Meal times where people talked and laughed and debated things. The only thing her dad ever debated was why his tea wasn't on the table at six and then he buried himself in *The Sun*. No wonder he didn't know anything and then there was Alf.

'Go on,' her dad had said, 'who else is going to look at you, you skinny bitch.'

The doctors at work were intelligent but she was invisible to them, except for Dr Jones. Not that they'd ever really spoken, but she sort of knew. He was different with her. He listened and looked. Looked like he was interested, not sexual. But now he'd let her down too.

'They'll be ready for you in five minutes,' Chrissie said, putting her head round the door.

'I know,' snapped Brenda.

'That's not going to help,' Chrissie said, 'I was only reminding you.'

'I know, but that's the third time I've been reminded. I'm not stupid. I can tell the time you know,' she said jabbing at her watch. Chrissie pursed her lips.

'OK then. Come in when you're ready.'

There were four people in the room. One she didn't know. Dr Hind turned to her.

'Hello Brenda. Have a seat. I think you know who everybody is except Leila, who will be observing today, if you have no objections.' Brenda shrugged.

'Can I take it then that you have no objections?'

'No, it's OK.'

'Good. Now,' she addressed the room, 'we increased your medication after we met last. How has that been suiting you, Brenda?'

'It makes me a bit sleepy, but it's OK.'

'Do you think it is making you more settled?'

Say yes, even if it isn't. Make them think you're doing well.

'Yes, I think so.'

'You haven't been mixing much and you didn't turn up for OT on Monday.'

'I don't like pottery. It's too messy. I went when we were doing painting.'

'It isn't really about liking it or not. We want you to fit in. Make more social contact. Have you made any friends here?'

You must be kidding, she wanted to say.

'I go into the day room. It's just that I get up before most of them and I like to listen to my radio.'

'OK, Brenda. Now what about the suicidal thoughts? Brenda took an overdose three weeks ago and spent the night here in hospital,' she told the room. 'What happened after that, Brenda? Perhaps you could tell us in your own words.'

Brenda frowned. *What was this about? They all knew. Was it for the benefit of that new person?*

'You don't have to say if you don't want to, but it might help to think about what happened.'

'I stayed in one night and they discharged me.'

'And then?' *She didn't want to say anything more.*

'Maybe it's easier if I explain. The reason that we are concerned and why you are here is that you did the same thing the next night, but this time it was more serious. It's lucky you've got Rob living next door.'

'Is it?' Brenda said staring at her. *That was a mistake.*

'Are you saying that you wish you had succeeded?'

'I might have done then, but I feel different now.'

'How different?'

'Well, I'm not going to do it again. I feel much better.'

'What was it that made you feel so desperate on that Monday, Brenda?'

'Oh, just something at work.'

She certainly wasn't going to tell them about that. She had gone to work. It had been just like any other day. She'd seen Dr Jones and he'd smiled at her and she was almost looking forward to starting the group on Friday. It had all seemed OK. They were very busy that day and at four o'clock she went to make some tea and when she got back Rosemary told her that Dr Petri wanted to see her. She went up to his office and he said he was glad she'd agreed to go to the group. Then he started saying that it was at Fairlawn's and they'd made an appointment for her on Wednesday to meet with Mr Patrick who would be running the group. She'd stared at him. What was he talking about? She was going to be in Dr Jones's group. That was the agreement. She'd said, 'I thought I was going to be in Dr Jones's group.' Dr Petri had smiled, a silly smile and said, no that wouldn't be possible. Hadn't Dr Jones made that clear? She'd felt tears. It wasn't fair. They'd tricked her. She didn't remember much else. She'd left the office and run down the stairs. There was a woman at the desk going on about needing to see somebody urgently. She was in the way of the door and she couldn't get in. All she wanted was to get her coat and go, so she'd pushed past her. She'd said, 'excuse me', but the woman started shouting and something had snapped and she started shouting back. Rosemary started pushing her towards the office, like she was just someone to be pushed around. The woman was shouting that she needed to see somebody now, and well, she didn't really remember what happened next. They said she hit the woman and that she was screaming at her. She remembered getting her coat and running out and Rosemary calling after her and her giving her the V-sign. After that she remembered walking round for a bit, then getting the bus and going to the chemist and buying some more paracetamol, not really sure whether she'd use them, but she'd have them anyway. What was the point? All that build up. A chance to be with him and all the time he didn't mean it. He'd betrayed her.

'Something at work?' Dr Hind was saying. 'Have you been able to talk about it to Chrissie or anybody?'

    'Oh yes,' said Brenda. 'I'm all right about it now.' She smiled round at them.

'Well, thanks Brenda. I think we'll keep your medication as it is for now. Thank you for coming. Have you any questions for us?'

'When can I go home?'

'Ah – I think we need to be sure that you are not going to harm yourself again.'

'But I won't. I'm OK,' Brenda protested.

'OK. We'll review it again at the next ward round. That will be,' she looked at her diary, 'this time next week. Thank you Brenda.'

Chapter 20

White berries

Brenda put a line through today's date. She'd been here for three weeks now. That was four ward rounds, eight OT sessions, four walks, in a line like they were idiots. God knows how many drugs pushing round her body, several attempts by Chrissie who was not too bad, and the new nurse, Chloe who was awful, to get her to 'talk'. She was beginning to realise that they were not going to let her go, not until they were good and ready. She was trapped. She had no autonomy. No power. It didn't matter what she wanted.

She'd gone along with what she could. She sat in the day room and tried to look interested. She could just about manage it when there was a reasonable programme on the telly but often there were arguments and the channel got changed to some quiz show or reality programme. Choosing to go to her room seemed the intelligent thing to do but they saw it as her being anti-social.

Her sister Sandra had come to the last ward round. Why did they call her, like she was the one who knew? They eyed each other. She wasn't going to behave as though Sandra was the sensible one and Sandra had put on a funny voice when she talked to the staff and Brenda wanted to laugh and ask her what she was doing. When they walked to her car, it was like she was still playing the game and she talked in a syrupy voice about her getting well and coming to stay with her and Stan when she came out. She nearly said, 'It's all right Sandra, they can't hear you anymore.' It was ridiculous. They'd never got on. This wasn't going to make it any better.

She'd stuck to the rules enough to be allowed to go for short walks by herself, as long as she didn't leave the grounds. That was something. If she could get out without Pauline trying to come with her, she could have a bit of independence, and, she wanted to look for the white berries.

It was only ward gossip, but what if it was true? Enid had said that there'd been a patient in last year and she had eaten them and it had worked. Brenda didn't really believe it. If that was true they'd have got rid of the plant. They just sent you to sleep, they said, and it didn't make you sick or hurt. If it was true, she could eat them with her cocoa and with the number of times they actually checked on them at night, actually opened the door and checked, it could all be over by the morning.

She'd had so much time to think about her life in here and they kept asking, how did she think she would manage when she got out? It was definite that she wouldn't be able to go back to 'The Firs' and that meant she might never see Dr Jones again. She wondered if he even knew she was here. One day she'd seen a car like his, parked near the building and a man who looked a bit like him and she thought, yes, for a moment she did think, he's come to visit me. He's come to say it was a mistake, make her his special patient and take her out of here. Maybe, feeling she'd had a raw deal, he would take her home, even let her stay at his house.

But it wasn't him. Not a bit like him in fact. No, Dr Jones had let her down like all the others. She walked past the boarded-up church and took the path to the left. Not many people went down here. It didn't look as if it went anywhere and just led to the wire fence by the houses at the end of the grounds. The gardens were full of bright plastic toys. Normal people with normal lives lived in those new houses, but they disappeared quickly enough if they saw one of them approaching.

The grounds were more overgrown here. There was litter and a broken trolley up-ended on the bank. It must have been a garden once. There were laurel bushes and some roses gone wild and a birch tree and, at the end, pink rhododendrons. The path almost disappeared and the laurel was thicker here but then she saw, hidden under the spotty camouflage, a small bush covered in white berries. Her heart quickened. Not since she had been admitted three weeks ago had anything excited her as much. She looked round. Nobody was in sight. She went up to the bush. Closer to, she could see that the berries were over their best. Many of them had burst and she could see brownish seeds and a sort of ooze leaking out. That's what they'd called them – slime berries. Taking a tissue from her bag she began to pick some of the best ones, the ones without blemish. She didn't know how many she would need. She counted them as she picked. When she had picked fifteen, she wrapped the tissue around them and put them carefully in her bag.

At the door, she met Chrissie coming out. She must be going off duty. Brenda felt a tiny stab of sadness. She might not see her again and she had been kind and interested.

'Hi Brenda. You look better. I'll see you tomorrow. Don't do anything I wouldn't do.'

'Bye Chrissie,' said Brenda sadly. 'Enjoy your evening. Thanks,' she added.

'Thanks for what? It's nice to see you looking happier. Bye.'

Brenda watched her walk to the car park. She almost wanted to call out stop, talk to me, tell me if it's right but she didn't. She went to her room and put the berries at the back of the cupboard and put her box with the Vecpoint pen and the two paper clips from his desk that she'd worn on a black jungle lace around her neck, and put her green jumper in front of them.

Chapter 21

Jessica's return

The train ploughed on. The carriage had six white leather seats. They travelled at speed, yet seemed to stand still. She didn't want to go but knew there was no choice.

When the train stopped she got out. A tall figure with neatly folded wings was waiting for her. He was white except for his gleaming black wings. He stretched out his hand. He turned and she followed. He indicated a white carriage. Two white stallions pawed the ground noiselessly. She stretched up and was in the trap. Instantly, he was beside her. The horses arched their necks and moved off. She looked at him and, sensing her gaze, he turned to her. His eyes were blue but transparent. Behind them she could see the clouds.

Ahead, she knew, was the gateway but she could see nothing but the white landscape. She thought of Drew but already the memory was fading and could not be recalled. She tried to picture his face. In spite of the white fur coat she was cold. She opened her mouth to scream but the word was snatched from her mouth. The horses sped on. She could sense the gate ahead. She knew it would be beautiful carved white marble. It began to snow. The horses slowed a little, ploughing on through the powdery swirls. She could not see ahead. Her companion was lost to view but she knew he was there. Knew he would stay until they reached the gate.

They burst out of the snow onto a glittering landscape. Blinding shafts of sunlight illuminated the plateau as far as she could see. Ahead was the gate. She looked at the man but he looked straight ahead. The horses were rushing now. Charging onwards. The gate was getting closer.

Images flashed passed her but so quickly that she couldn't retain them. A face, a scene, a tree and house, a lake. She gasped but it was gone. The man turned and looked at her. His eyes, opaque now, reflected images of towns and rivers and people.

'What...?' she cried. But her words were lost in the wind. They were hurtling on.

The gate loomed up. Abruptly the horses stopped. The man was beside the trap, helping her down. Tears froze on her cheeks. He took her hand, helped her down. Then he was back in the trap. The horses pawed the ground.

'Please,' she stammered, 'don't leave me.'

'Goodbye and good luck,' he said. The horses turned and he was gone. She looked around. Ahead was the gateway. Without a sound the gate opened and she walked towards it.

Chapter 22
Eva

There was the usual junk mail and two letters on the mat. One, Ash could see, was from Tom and the other with the Swedish stamp was probably from Eva. After her text he'd been expecting a letter from her but if she'd been in Finland or had to go up to Lulea, she wouldn't write till she got back. He filled the kettle and sat down to read the letters. The one from Eva had two photographs tucked inside. Eva, in a woolly hat, smiled out at him and in the second she stood with Britt, the sled and the dogs yoked ready for a trip, behind them. Both women looked happy.

The toast popped up and still reading, he poured water into the teapot, thinking about how far apart he and Eva were. Her world with months of snow and cold, long distances covered with skies, a life that gave a common sense pragmatism, so different from his world of emotions and unfulfilled needs. He put the toast onto a plate.

The letter was chatty with delightful idiosyncratic spelling, full of news about her work and evenings out with friends. He knew most of the people she wrote about but any mention of Ulf gave his heart a twist. 'Ulf is a married colleague,' she'd said. The last paragraph said that she could not be back for a couple of months and he suddenly felt very sad. This had been a long break.

Both Lapland and Eva had been a surprise. The few days with friends in Stockholm included a trip to Lapland. Across a frozen lake they came across a group of people in middle of a frozen lake. They lay on reindeer skins fishing with reindeer antlers through circular holes cut in the ice. He was invited to have a go. He knew only two Lappish words yet these men and women spoke immaculate English. 'We learn it in school,' they said with a shrug. The ice was thicker than he had imagined and at the bottom of the curious ice tunnel, fish could be seen darting back and forth. The skill was to drop the line when you saw the fish. Eva had laughed at his delight every time he caught one of the tiny fish.

He thought how attractive the people were with their unselfconscious clothes made for the climate. Eva wore a patterned woolly hat and reindeer skin boots. She gave him some dry gloves, smiling as she handed them to him. The gloves were warm from her hands. Later, he returned them, reluctantly.

In the evening they were taken to a wooden hall beside the frozen river for an opera recital by a local girl singer trained in Stockholm. It was bizarre but like everything, seemed quite natural. As they walked to the hall, from every house, people came out and Hamlin-like joined the crowd walking to the hall.

He'd never seen snow like it. Seeing a tree he liked, he'd stepped off the path and found himself waist deep in the softness. His companions were too polite to laugh. He saw reindeer herds and tipis and in the supermarket Sunni villagers in their embroidered red coats shopping for bread and milk and cut price offers.

At the opera, Eva seemed to be part of the organisation. There were too many people for him to do anything other than catch an occasional smile but he was very aware of her, searching for her, pleased when he located her, laughing, smiling, happy. How quickly she had got into his soul – already she was part of his life. She was friendly and easy with people. He could imagine healthy, robust sex with her.

Later, on the mountain road, the driver slammed on the brakes as an elk lazily crossed in front of them. If you hit one of them you don't have much car left, the driver said. The animal looked nonchalantly at them. It was very big and slightly unbelievable. Ulf, he remembered, had been there that evening too. He'd explained as they walked beside the frozen river, that the small neat buildings were for the bodies of those who died during the winter, stored until they could be buried in the thaw. It all felt like a bizarre distant dream.

He buttered his toast slowly, fetched a spoon for the marmalade and sipping his tea thoughtfully. Tom's letter was just one page, which was unusual. He was still bored, still doing his best to keep occupied. He hoped Ash could come and see him soon and Claire's visit had been a success. He'd been really pleased to see her and glad that she was OK with him. It had been weird to see how the men looked at her and made him realise how attractive she was. He still didn't have a release date but he had been told he should hear something soon. That was all.

Ash put down the letter, frowning a little. Nothing really to worry him but Tom's letters were usually two or three pages long with drawings in the margins and full of his thoughts and ideas. This was flat and factual. He must try and get to see him this week or next. Geraldine had not phoned this week. Probably not contacting him was her way of suggesting that he ought to be doing more.

He put the letters back into the envelope and propped the smiling picture of Eva against the vase of white nettles and buttercups he'd collected at the weekend.

Chapter 23
Carl

Carl could not speak, it seemed. The group had been running five weeks now and as far as Leila could remember, he had still not said a word. If he had a chance, he sat next to her. He seemed to find the silences especially difficult and after the third session, she'd asked Ash whether they should try to help him

'When he's ready, he will say what he needs to,' Ash had said. 'At the moment, it's enough that he's here.'

Steph was clearly fed up with him and last week Peter had asked him a few questions but Carl just looked up, smiled, blinked and then looked down again. The group, now anticipating that he wouldn't say anything, had begun to ignore him. Leila felt this was not a good thing and would smile or look encouragingly at him if he ever looked up.

Sometimes she saw Ash looking at him. She'd even wondered if Carl could speak, but Ash had told her that when he'd been on his own with him, he had spoken, and though almost monosyllabic, he had managed to say quite forcibly that he wanted to come to the group and, unlike Linda, he hadn't missed a session. She was developing a real warmth towards him and felt protective when Steph said something sharply to him. He seemed terrified of Steph and stood back or walked quickly to the door if he found himself anywhere near her, and he never sat next to her if he had a choice.

Leila hadn't realised that she would develop such strong feelings towards the group members. Ash treated them all with the same respect and interest but she wondered whether he too felt warmer to some than others. She wondered what she would do if she didn't like somebody. She asked him about it.

'Do you feel differently about some of them?' he'd asked and she had answered, telling him about her feelings and not hearing about his. 'Wait till you start to dream about them,' Ash had said, and smiled.

She had started to look forward to the group sessions and her liking and respect for Ash was increasing. He seemed infinitely fair and always had time for her questions. He looked quite tired sometimes, she noticed. She made the occasional observation, which Ash treated in the same respectful way, but it often sounded stupid or obvious the minute it was out of her mouth and put her off. She understood how Carl felt.

Watching Carl, Ash thought of the inarticulate part of himself, the times when he could not express what he felt. Painful conversations with Geraldine came to mind. Of all the sadness he felt for their failed marriage, their inability to communicate had been the worst for him. Certainly his withdrawal into himself had often been angry. Was Carl's muteness angry?

He watched Carl struggle in the group. Sometimes he would look up for several minutes, staring hard at the person speaking, waiting for a pause, almost shaking with the wish to say something, then somebody would cut in and down would go his head again. The only parts of him that talked were his feet. They jiggled most of the time. Would he be able to get the feeling from his feet to his mouth before he burst? Ash feared that before he managed to do this, he would give up, and not come back.

He thought of their first meeting. He'd been surprised to find him in the waiting room with his mother. Throughout the interview it had been almost impossible to stop his mother speaking for him. At the second interview, Ash had suggested that he might like to come in by himself, and Carl had nodded and the mother had sat back down, shocked and surprised. If they didn't let him speak on his own now, would they really be helping him? Steph wasn't giving him much of a chance. She simply ignored him and never looked at him. Even Norma, well meaning as she was, wasn't helping. She too, clearly found the silences difficult, but couldn't let them be so that as Carl geared himself to speak, she filled the space.

This week, Ash again watched him trying to summon up the courage to speak. He found himself holding his breath, willing him to manage, but in the end looking away. He had to believe that the continual frustration would eventually propel Carl into speaking. If he was rescued now, he would again be reliant on somebody else. He could wait, and if everybody else could, he felt sure Carl would eventually find his voice.

Chapter 24

Genesis

Jessica circled, less disembodied but still invisible. It was a small semi-detached house in a row of similar houses that backed onto the railway line. She moved to the back of the house. Each house had a narrow garden leading to a path that ran parallel to the railway bank. Some gardens were neat with well tended grass and a few had borders with pretty flowers. One had the beginnings of some decking, and another had a hole recently dug for a pond; the blue shell glowing green with mould where the water had long since drained from it.

The garden of number twenty-three had a rectangle of tall weeds, a pile of rubble, a wheelbarrow on its side, some planks of wood and a pot with an almost dead geranium; one bright red flower stoically remaining. An air of neglect and despair pervaded.

The back door of the house opened and a man in a vest came out. He coughed and spat. His hair was slicked back as if he had just washed or showered and he wore slippers. There was a tinkling sound from the railway line and Jessica moved behind the fence uncertain at the strange noise. The noise increased in strength and then bursting forth a train thundered past shaking the ground. The leaves of the geranium shuddered with the rhythm of the rails and as the train shot onwards, sucking the air behind it, a brown leaf detached itself and fell to join the carpet of leaves surrounding the stem. The man looked at his watch, nodded, stubbed out his cigarette and went indoors.

Jessica moved up the street past the gardens and back along the front of the houses. Here and there attempts had been made at modernizing or improving the houses. There was a brightly painted bird in stained glass in the inset of a door and one house had rows of hanging baskets with bright, clashing petunias whose busyness made her breathless.

As she approached number twenty-three, the man, now dressed to go out, shut the front door with a bang. He got into a battered red car and drove off, the exhaust sending out clouds of uncombusted petrol fumes.

With the house now empty, Jessica entered. A smell of cigarettes, bad cooking and dirt pervaded and everything had an air of poverty and scrimping. In the sitting room a faded sofa and an armchair faced a grate filled with cigarette packets and butts. Newspapers were strewn around the room. On the table, covered with an oilskin cloth, stood a beer bottle, a glass and a dirty plate. On the sideboard, in a once silver frame, was a photograph of a woman in a neat, blue dress. She was not smiling. One curtain was still drawn and the other was hanging off its hooks. A dirty net curtain helped to keep out the only light from the small window. There was a kitchen to the left but Jessica did not venture in.

So this was where Brenda grew up. Upstairs were two bedrooms. One, whose squalid contents signaled the man's occupancy, had a large unmade bed. In the other, under a covering of dust, were two single beds and a dressing table with a broken drawer containing a pink brush with hairs, a notebook and, on the bed, a doll with staring eyes. On the wall were two posters. The whole house had an air of sadness, as if it had seen little love or fun. Jessica left the house, impatient to see where Brenda was now.

Brenda was very ill. The room was shaded and there was a plastic jug of water with a blue lid on a locker and a bowl of fruit. A white bedcover covered the bed. Jessica could hear chatter from a corridor but the room was quiet. In the bed the pale face of Brenda, eyes closed, lay still, the sheets pulled across her chest as if she had not moved since the bed was made around her. Jessica moved across the room. Brenda was so still and pale that for a moment she wondered if she was dead. Closer to, she could feel the shallow breath from the slightly parted lips. Her charge was evidently quite ill. What, she wondered, had happened to Brenda between the sad life in the terraced house and this ill shadow of a person in the bed before her?

Chapter 25

Steph's words burned into Norma's mind and all week she smarted when she thought about it and no amount of telling herself about sticks and stones helped. She had wanted to join the group for self-improvement and to be a better person. At her interview she'd said to Dr Jones that she felt her experience of community life would make her a good group member and he had looked grave and nodded slowly. She added that she felt she was a good listener and was sure she could help the others in the group and might even be quite good at it, if she allowed a little pride. He had asked her what she wanted from the group. She said she thought that, though she hadn't lived in the outside world, she knew enough about it from the charitable work they'd all done, but Steph's remark ... Was it true? It was so unfair. She wanted to be kind and support people but the words had hurt so, and these were feelings she hadn't experienced much before.

After that meeting, a loneliness crept over her that she hadn't experienced since the early convent days. She had few doubts about her decision to leave the Order and, with so much opposition put in her way, the battle had preoccupied her and left her little time for regrets. Her decision was courageous. Even the Reverend Mother, when she'd got over some of her anger, had acknowledged that. She had been regarded as intrepid in the work she had volunteered for. She could be strong, but could she take on Steph? What she had said was cruel and unjust. 'You're just a sycophantic yes-man'. Norma was determined to say something about it though the thought of the confrontation made her heart pound. Even calling her man and not woman, she didn't understand.

And this group was so bewildering. They seemed to be being encouraged to look at negative things all the time, to acknowledge feelings like anger and envy that her convent life had taught her to suppress. She liked Dr Jones and respected him, but he puzzled her. When she was being supportive of a group member, glancing at him for approval, he often frowned or looked at the floor.

She liked Peter, and Carl so clearly wanted to speak. In one session she had really tried to help him, asking him things and suggesting that he didn't have to say much and then – that was one of the times she looked up expecting Dr Jones's encouraging smile and instead he looked, well, almost cross. What was wrong with trying to help? Wasn't that what they were here for? She didn't find it difficult to speak in the group, why shouldn't she help Carl?

She was the first to arrive as usual. Nobody was at the desk. She'd had a cup of tea with her breakfast and didn't need another. She found a glass and had a drink of water. She heard somebody behind her and Linda appeared in the doorway.

'Hello. How are you?' she said brightly, pleased to see somebody else.

'Hi,' said Linda flatly. She heard the group room door open and through the half-open door saw people leaving. A woman came into the kitchen and started to fill the kettle. She looked as if she'd been crying. Norma smiled at her sympathetically but this was met with a scowl. The earlier group seemed to have left the room. She waited a moment, then feeling uncomfortable, she went to the group room.

A woman was putting papers into a briefcase. Norma retreated, nearly colliding with Linda. The woman gave her an irritated look, closed the briefcase and walked quickly out of the room without a further glance at Norma. The woman was slim with sleek black hair. Arrogance surrounded her and Norma hated her instantly. Such a strong feeling. It shocked her. What was happening to her? It was as if all the rules were different.

For once time was going slowly. She kept glanced at the clock. Leila's smile when she arrived had helped. Perhaps she would be an ally. Steph was late. Relieved at first, Norma then felt disappointed. The adrenalin was up and now she wanted to get on with it.

Steph arrived ten minutes late, disgruntled and surly. Norma felt anxious again. Steph was wearing a maroon beret and nice boots. She could be very attractive if she smiled. Involuntarily Norma had smiled at her when she arrived but it was greeted with the usual indifference. She thought she would wait a few minutes. Then Linda said, 'I didn't want to come today,' looking at Dr Jones and then at Leila. Norma's heart quickened at this insubordination. Dr Jones didn't look offended, just curious. Nobody said anything.

'I don't enjoy these sessions,' Linda continued. 'I don't understand what we are supposed to be doing.' Again nobody said anything. It was intolerable.

'I don't always want to come either,' said Norma, 'but I'm glad when I get here.' She sensed, rather than heard, Steph's barely suppressed sigh. Bravely she stared at her. Steph looked away.

'I had a bad dream last night,' Peter said. 'I was on this boat and I wanted to get off but I knew I couldn't swim. I can swim – just in the dream, I couldn't.' They turned to look at him.

'Peter, maybe we could look at your dream in a minute, if you still want to but, I am curious about why it was difficult for Linda to come to the group today,' said Dr Jones.

'I don't see the point,' Linda trailed off.

'You don't have to come,' said Steph. 'If it's not doing you any good, what's the point?'

'I know I don't have to come, but I thought it would make me better ... but I'm just as depressed as ever,' Linda said.

'Maybe it's the time of year. Lots of people suffer from SAD,' consoled Norma.

'For Christ's sake Norma,' Steph burst out, 'you're doing it again!' Caught in the headlights, trapped, cornered, Norma felt the pistons engage.

'Doing what, exactly?' she said, turning to face her.

'Placating – making noises – being so bloody nice.'

'It's better than saying the unkind things you say,' she retorted.

'At least they're true.'

'So's my concern for Linda.'

'No it's not. It's just to make you feel better. You're no more concerned for Linda than a bar of soap. At least I say what I feel.'

Dr Jones cut in. 'If we could think for a minute about what Linda is finding difficult it might help everybody. I'm sure there are times when all of you don't want to be somewhere or do something and how you each manage that might help us to understand it.'

'I'm glad you're here,' said Carl in a quiet voice. 'You're pretty and you have a nice smile ... and I would miss you if you weren't here.' He looked down, his face quite red now. There was a silence. Steph looked nonplussed.

'I would be sorry too,' said Peter. Norma wanted to say she would too but conscious of Steph, she only smiled.

'I missed you the other week when you weren't here,' Carl continued. It was amazing. Here was Carl who never said anything, saying something surprising.

'Perhaps you're realizing that you are becoming important to each other,' said Dr Jones, 'and whether you are here or not affects you and the group.' That's true, Norma thought. She looked round at the others, meeting their glances but not needing to say anything. Perhaps support was not always about words. She felt a feeling of warmth towards the group and catching Steph's eye, she held her stare. Was there even a slight smile?

'Can I tell you about my dream now?' said Peter.

Chapter 26

Saturday

The phone rang. It was Saturday. Ash put down the paper reluctantly.

'Tom's got his release date,' Geraldine said. 'His parole meeting's next week and they should tell him then. He tried to phone you but you were out.' Always the underlying accusation, but she sounded more animated than he'd heard her for a long time. He sometimes forgot what a strain it was on her.

'He wanted to speak to you because one of us needs to give an address for him to be released to.'

'Oh. Does he want to come to you?'

'Well, yes, or to you.' Her tone was irritated. 'What about him coming to you?' she said. 'He can come here, of course, but with the wedding and everything, well, I thought perhaps it would be good if he came to you initially.' The word *good* was not lost on Ash.

'Of course,' said Ash, 'if that's what he wants.'

'He doesn't really mind,' she snapped. 'It's just that he's got to give somewhere. It will hold up his release otherwise. Can you phone the prison and leave a message? Speak to that Belling guy who's dealing with his case. If I hear anything more, I'll let you know. You've got plenty of room after all. It'll be good for both of you like this.'

Ash put down the phone. The relief was enormous. Tom was coming out. He hoped they wouldn't mess him about and change their minds. Clearly the guarantee of an address would be important.

But after the initial relief, another thought came into his head, making him feel ashamed. In a few weeks, Eva might be here. Did he really want his adolescent son cramping his style? He looked round at the ordered neatness of the flat and he knew that the tidiness and order of his single life would be disrupted in a way that he would find difficult.

Chapter 27

Ash surveyed the scene. There was a half-full cup and a plate on top of a pile of papers. The cushions of the settee had been piled up at one end and the rug was on the floor. The vase of tulips had been pushed to the edge of the table. Such small changes but they irritated. The door of Tom's room was shut. His trainers were outside the door, ending the trail of garments leading from the hall.

He'd heard Tom come in but had not noticed the time. All he knew was that it was late. When he got back this evening, Tom would probably be out or lolling in front of the telly. At least when Tom was asleep, there was not the continual low thud of his music. He seemed to be making no effort to get a job since his release. Ash took the dishes into the kitchen. Tom had seemed so shocked when he came out, subdued and a bit lost.

It was a long time since they'd spent any time together and, conscious of what he'd been through, Ash had been pleased to have the chance to look after him. Tom said he'd contacted the local AA group and was going to meetings but he didn't want to talk. This was disappointing but often by the time Ash got back from work, he was tired and relieved to find Tom out. He hoped though, for both their sakes, that Tom would find his own place soon but first he needed a job. Lending him more money wouldn't help. These were practical worries but Ash felt unease under it all. He didn't know if he could trust him. Had he really given up? He'd found himself looking for telltale signs; alcohol on his breath and twice he'd searched his room for hidden bottles. Tom was a smoker so there were the usual trappings, whether there was anything more, Ash couldn't worry about. He didn't allow him to smoke in the flat and he hadn't smelt anything. He knew enough about alcoholism to recognise that Tom needed to quit completely. Half measures wouldn't work and without the help of others, he would not succeed. Tom's adolescent sleeping pattern had returned, late mornings and late nights, and though probably a reaction, it did not bode well. It would be good to have Geraldine's view on how Tom was when she came to supper tonight. Perhaps Tom would talk then.

He picked up the papers and re-arranged the cushions on the sofa. The packet of cigarette papers he found under one, he put inside one of Tom's trainers. Wiping the table, he put the tulips back in the centre of the table and folded the rug. In the kitchen he floured sole filets and put them on a plate in the fridge. He sliced potatoes ready to sauté and quickly made a dressing with mayonnaise, yogurt and horseradish. It was still important to him that he was seen to maintain standards in front of Geraldine. He left for work hoping that the flat would be as he'd left it when he got back.

Tom was not in when he returned from work and with some relief, Ash poured himself a whiskey and put on an Elgar CD. The flat was almost as he had left it. Tom's door was shut but the trainers had gone and the clothes had disappeared from the hall. Ash showered and settled to read the rugby report. He was watching the news when Geraldine rang the doorbell.

They were never easy, these meetings they had. She wore a smart suit and she looked and smelled expensive and she had that just showered appearance that he had always liked. All this flashed through his mind as she stood framed in the doorway, the sun catching the blond of her hair, thought the fact that they had ever had a sex life seemed inconceivable to him now.

At eight o'clock Tom had not returned. With the television on in the background, they had chatted superficially about Tom, and about Claire's wedding. He'd hoped to discuss his concerns about Tom but quickly sensed Geraldine's feeling that he should be being more directive with him.

At nine he decided to start the supper. He felt nervous and what would normally be an easy meal, became problematic under her scrutiny. He was so aware of the many triggers that could start an argument and he deliberately left the television on as it was showing a programme he knew she liked. Recalling the years of treading on eggshells, he felt relief that he no longer had to bear this discomfort.

Geraldine ate with relish, appreciating the food. Cooking had been a point of contact for them.

By ten Tom had not returned and Geraldine, irritated now, said she could not wait any longer. 'Who knows what time he will come in?'

Ash watched the ten o'clock news and as it came to an end, he heard the key in the door. Tom came in and loitered near the door. Ash ignored him and went into the kitchen. Tom flopped down on the sofa.

'Hi Dad … what's wrong?'

'Your mother was here,' Ash said.

'Oh – is she OK?'

'Is she OK? You were supposed to be here. She came for supper.'

'Oh – shit.' Tom looked genuinely surprised. 'Was I? I'm sorry. I forgot. I'll phone her in a minute.'

'It's too late to phone now. She'll be in bed. Where were you? Why couldn't you phone?'

'I've lost my mobile.'

'How? Where did you lose it?' Tom shrugged. He got up and went into the kitchen.

'Do you want a coffee?' Tom said, lurching towards the cupboard. He reached for a cup and the jar of coffee. Ash watched as he spilled coffee over the table, then opened the fridge and took out some milk.

'Aren't you going to put the kettle on?' Ash said coldly.

'Oh – yeah …' said Tom smiling.

'You're drunk,' said Ash. 'After all you've been through, you're bloody drunk again.' He snatched the spoon from Tom's hand and put on the kettle. 'Your mother came round specially to see you to sort out what you're going to do and you come back drunk. I bet you've not even been going to your meetings.'

'I did go Dad but well … I will stop, really. It's just so …'

'So bloody what? You've lost your licence. You've been in prison and you've lost your mobile. What more do you want? What are you doing with your life?'

'Hey, steady Dad. It's only a drink and it's not as if you don't.'

'That's not the point. I work and pay the bills and this is my flat and you're my guest.'

'Guest – I'm your bloody son.'

'Then act like it. Get a job. Get sober. This has gone too far!'

'I'll go if it's so difficult having me here,' he said.

'Where would you go?'

'Somewhere … I've got friends.'

'What – other drunken sods. How will that help?'

'It probably won't but at least I don't get the third degree whenever I get back. I hate it here anyway. It's so neat – like a woman – I feel watched all the time. It's as bad as prison.'

'OK. Go then! Find your own way.'

'OK. I will. I'll go in the morning – if that's all right with you,' he added in a sarcastic tone. He picked up his sweatshirt and went to his room, slamming the door.

Ash regretted the words as soon as they were out of his mouth. He didn't sleep well and Tom was not up when he left for work. Several times his thoughts returned to the conversation. There were so many ways he could have handled it besides getting angry. So many better ways of doing it.

When he got home Tom's door was wide open, and his things were gone. On the table was a note.

Sorry if I've been a nuisance – can't live up to your standards. See you Dad. Love Tom.

There was no forwarding address and without the mobile, Ash wondered how he could contact him.

Geraldine had been strangely calm when he phoned to tell her about Tom.

'What happened?' she asked.

'He came back at about ten thirty saying he had forgotten you were coming to supper – completely drunk.' There was an intake of breath.

'You had wondered hadn't you?' she said with surprising sympathy.

'Yes, but I was shocked. He seemed so casual about it. I don't think he's been going to the meetings or anything. I'm afraid I lost it.' There was a pause. He waited, expecting the usual tirade.

Instead Geraldine said, 'I think maybe it had to happen.'

'You do?' said Ash.

'I don't think he's ready to give up yet. I think prison frightened him but he still thinks he is in control. It may be a good thing that he's gone and has to stand on his own.' A wave of relief flooded Ash. He could feel his animosity melting.

'It's good to have your support,' he said. 'I've been feeling bad all day.' Again there was a pause.

'I've been going to a couple of support meetings,' Geraldine said. 'They say this all the time.'

'Say what?'

'Oh, you know … about rescuing. I think we've been doing that for years. They say it doesn't help them.'

'What do they say we should do?'

'Make him face it. They would say he hasn't reached rock bottom yet and every time we make it easy for him, he won't face it.'

'That's pretty tough. So if he wants to come back, what should I do?'

'Don't let him.'

'What if he contacts you?'

'I won't let him either.' There was a long pause.

'Do you think they are right?'

'I know they are.'

'It's easy when it's other people. I'm worried though. I'd just like to know where he is – oh – and he's lost his mobile.' There was a tut from the other end of the phone. 'It's good to be doing this together,' said Ash.

'Yes'. There was a silence, both lost in their own reflections. 'So – we're agreed to be tough with him then,' Geraldine said. Ash sensed the call was at an end.

'Yes … but let's keep in touch. With anything that happens, I mean.'

'Of course,' Geraldine said sharply. 'Bye Ash.' Ash put down the phone surprisingly warmed by her use of his name.

Chapter 28

A break

Ash flicked through the pile of letters on his desk. He opened the drawer and took out the letter opener. A blackbird trilled outside the window capturing his attention. He opened the first letter. It was a further notification about the Greek conference next month. He glanced at the list of speakers. The keynote speaker was Dr Louis, his old tutor. That would be worth listening to and it would be good to see him again. *There will be a panel of other speakers who will respond to Dr Louis's talk* he read. *The supporting speakers are Hannah Little* – what was her connection with this lot? – *Barbara Scott and Caroline Mayfield.* What a strange coincidence. The four day timetable was enclosed and papers were invited. He'd missed the deadline. He put the notice down and opened the rest of his post.

Later in the morning, he looked at the invitation again. It wasn't that he really wanted to go to the conference, but a couple of weeks on a Greek island might be just what he needed. He visualised the sea, the easy days, the lack of responsibility. He looked at the flyer again. It was strange to have three people who he had history with, all speaking at the same conference. There was a knock at the door reminding him that it was time for his next appointment. He pushed the letter to one side and reached for his jacket.

* * *

At about five thirty, Ash closed and locked the filing cabinet. He tidied his desk, poured the last of the water from his glass onto the plant on his desk. He straightened the in-tray and put the pens together neatly. He sat down to put the stapler and scissors away. He picked up the flyer again and put it into his briefcase aware of some excitement at the thought of a possible break. He could look up flights tonight.

At the intersection there was the usual rush hour hold-up. How would it feel listening to Hannah and would she feel uncomfortable him being there? They had been pretty friendly before last year's conference. They'd both been on their own that year – so many of them were. He'd even considered a holiday fling. She was attractive with a lot of energy and fun and there was clearly an interest. He imagined she had a man in her life but then he had Eva. It needn't be serious. When he'd found her crying on that second day, he'd felt very rejected when his concern had been firmly pushed away, and he imagined he had misread the signs and felt a little foolish. When later, she'd teamed up with Bernice he'd been pleased … pleased that she had found someone to talk to if it couldn't be him.

One day he'd decided to walk to the cove beyond the rocks. He felt a contentment he got only when he was away from home and work, both in time and distance. The scenery was beautiful and he was experiencing again his love of Greece. He was at the far end of the cove, clambering over the rocks when, just behind a large boulder, he saw Hannah and Bernice, topless and in an embrace that was more than sisterly.

Shocked, he stepped back, almost falling. He hoped they hadn't seen him but clearly they had, and sprang apart guiltily. He'd been mildly shocked and unsettled. Over the next few days, he saw Hannah a couple of times but neither said anything and it felt as if something had been severed. He wanted to say, it was OK with him; that he was glad she had found someone. But he had been shocked. Shocked that he had never questioned her sexuality. How would he feel listening to her talking at the conference on literature and psychosis?

He pressed the fob on his car keys and the neat black car winked its recognition. The car park was dark and only a few cars were still there. He indicated left, pulled out and turned towards home.

He wondered too about Barbara Scott, the other speaker. How had she got so elevated as to be a speaker? This was probably unfair, but he was tired. It was only a couple of years, since she'd come to him for an assessment. True, she was already quite an established writer, an interesting woman, but in quite a mess. Her recovery must have been pretty remarkable if she was now able to lecture to an audience of practitioners.

He caught the corner shop just as it was closing. He bought milk and bread, a mango and four tomatoes. He put them on the passenger seat and pulled out into the main road.

At home he cooked a simple meal. Steak, fried potatoes and salad. He opened a bottle of white wine and watched the end of the tennis.

Chapter 29

Greece

Mamma was taking the two dogs for a walk. The old dog padding along and the little one, subdued for once, walked behind. The fronds of the bamboo umbrellas fluttered in the breeze. Small waves lapped the shore in parallel. Across the water, the mountain looked bold, the morning light giving it a particular serenity. Cats stalked the beach, bizarre amongst the sun beds, and bees swarmed round the orange hibiscus. A mangey cat, watched by a tabby with a swollen eye, sipped water from the puddle left by the tap. He dropped a piece of cheese onto the floor hoping that one of them would get it before the birds. Life here, for animals and humans, had sometimes to be fought for.

Ash swam strongly. He was glad he'd stayed on after the conference. The taverna was familiar and friendly and a week in the sun had strengthened him, but still the sadness remained. He swam towards the horizon. The sea was soft and containing and he felt free. But what was the deep sadness? Could a poor start ever be repaired and what about his own parenting? How well had he done with that? A dead daughter, a son a drunk, a failed marriage. Only Claire was relatively normal. He swam with deep strokes. Maybe he'd done his best. Sasha had been a loved child. Her death had nearly broken them all. Tom had found relief in drink but now he had a chance to turn his life around and Claire, well, he needed one relatively normal child. Perhaps after all, it had not been so bad.

The water was a little colder here. It caressed his body. There was no doubt that the sun and sea heightened sensuality. He missed Eva. Would she ever commit and was that what he wanted?

He turned over on his back and looked at the shore realising how far he had swum. He needed to turn back. Now facing the shore he seemed to be swimming against the tide. He swam strongly but seemed to be making little progress. He might phone Geraldine later and see if she had heard from Tom, though they didn't encourage contact for the first few weeks. The shore seemed just as far away and he realised that his arms were quite tired. He changed to a crawl, hoping to move more quickly towards the shore. He felt a slight panic. Had he swum out too far? There were few people on this part of the beach. He could just disappear. Apart from the discomfort of drowning, the thought was strangely comforting. His turn of speed had brought him closer to the shore and returning to a gentler stroke, he turned on his back using his hand to paddle. Soon he could stand, sand soft under his feet, warm and safe.

Today he went to a different part of the beach and a different taverna. Blue-checked cloths covered the tables. He chose one facing the sea and ordered a beer. The island's peace was beginning to permeate him. Later he would walk along the beach, read, and tonight eat at his favourite taverna. Most of the people from the conference had gone and he was pleased to have the extra time on his own.

This beach was hardly more than a hundred yards from his usual one but something was quite different. A young man, who he had quickly identified as special, was half hiding behind a tree, his back to the café. He was struggling to take off his swimming trunks under a towel. Ash averted his eyes, but short of moving chairs, it was hard to ignore him. With difficulty the young man struggled to hold up the towel and remove the trunks. He stopped every so often with the effort, leaving the small towel revealing his bottom. Suddenly the towel fell to the ground, revealing all. The young man looked surprised, bent down to pick up the towel, his bottom in full view. Gently amused Ash changed seats so he faced away from him. Now dressed, the young man went to join the other groups on the beach.

A youngish man was putting up umbrellas. He and a woman with red hair seemed to be in charge An older woman with tyres of fat circling her legs, leaned on a stick talking animatedly to three others under an umbrella. Many of the people in the party, he noticed, were elderly. A man with a huge belly walked down the café steps making his ungainly way across the beach. He waddled into the sea where he became a beautiful porpoise, swimming with grace and style.

Behind him, voices and laughter heralded a thin man with long grey hair and jeans, wearing a headdress of orange hibiscus and followed by a small entourage who danced along behind him. Fascinated Ash watched him, convinced now that he was witnessing an outing from the local hospital. The man with the headdress and his entourage danced towards a car. Their driver was probably going to take them home, Ash thought, but then saw that the man with the orange headdress was getting into the driver's seat.

Ash paid and walked back along the beach. The scene he had witnessed strangely disturbed him. Perhaps it was something of the gentle bizarreness of the outing that touched a feeling of unreality that matched his own.

He walked along the water's edge, enjoying the feel of the wet sand and waves splashing over his feet. It could be assumed, he reflected, that at any given time his mental state would be a step ahead of his patients but how true was that? He left the beach and took the path up to the village. He walked quite quickly aware of the heat of the sun on his hatless head, but after a few yards the chest pain returned.

He was used to interpreting physical symptoms as unconscious manifestations of inner distress. So, he had heart ache. What was that? He stopped under the shade of a fig tree. Who had his heart? The children and Eva, of course, but then an image of Renée came into his mind. What he wanted was comfort. Enveloping, cushiony comfort. How good it would be to meet her in the taverna and pour out his heart. But she was old, for Christ sake. Where did that thought come from? He felt shocked. He walked on. The sun beat down. He felt confused, unsettled. Sex and love. Lust and longing. He was on holiday. It was just his mind wandering.

In the midday haze a couple approached. She was slim with a bare torso and long hair. She was young enough to be his daughter but he was too weary to pull his eyes away from her attractiveness. It was just the aesthetic, he told himself. Beautiful proportions, like looking at a painting, but he knew he was rationalising. The idea of waking to see such a beautiful creature in bed beside him, having chosen him, found him viable, was better in its immediacy than an older woman's understanding. He longed to impress; to teach; to initiate. To have that adoration that belonged to youth and vigour.

He stopped again at a shaded place, disguising his aching chest by his studied viewing of the landscape. What would he do when he got to his room? Collapse probably. The rest of the day yawned ahead. He could sleep for a while and would enjoy that but the evening lay ahead like a chasm. He needed to eat, but alone? Why hadn't he asked Eva to come with him? In unfamiliar territory they could have enjoyed each other but he also knew that any time spent with her further committed him. Another couple passed him, the young woman unselfconscious, beautiful. An old man's dreams. He felt a touch of guilt at how quickly thoughts of Eva left him and how simple desire robbed him of his morality.

* * *

One day a cat died in the cobbled street outside his apartment. From his veranda he could look down the cobbled street to the café. The houses opposite were less than twelve metres away. The village was coming to life after the siesta and he could see the waitress setting out the tables.

At first he thought the cat was just enjoying a sunny spot. Its front and back legs were straight out as if it was enjoying the stretch. Then he noticed the tail quivering and he saw that the head was jerking and there was a red mark near its mouth. It was a pale ginger-and-white tabby, thin and delicate like all the Greek cats. Still not quite sure whether the cat was ill or whether it had a mannerism, he stood watching. The convulsions were now more violent. Nobody was about and he didn't know if he should go down. If it was ill what could he do? Was it a pet or just one of the many cats that survived on the streets?

The cat was stiller now. Clearly it was dying or even dead. He stood watching, continually thinking it had died until another convulsion shook it. Now convinced that it was near death, Ash wished that it would happen quickly. He wondered why he continued to watch it. Perhaps it was because it was so alone. Just down the street there was bustle and noise but here, this sad little drama was taking place, witnessed only by him. With a last convulsion the cat shook and was still. Ash knew this was the moment. Still nobody came. Absent for once, were the man and woman who usually sat on chairs on the corner, their grandson playing at their feet.

Reluctantly Ash went inside, returning to the balcony every time he heard voices or noises outside, but each time the noise came from further down the street. He thought of Sasha's cat, so lovingly buried in the shoebox in the garden. The care in preparing the box helping the little girl deal with her pet's death.

He heard voices, loud voices and a commotion. He moved to go and look but then returned to his chair. There were more excited voices and after a while the sound of water splashing and brushing noises. The sad little end he had witnessed stayed in his mind and he was glad not to have seen the probable picking up of the cat by its tail, to be shoved into a bag and deposited with the rubbish at a suitable place. His heart stayed with the little creature. Hurt, dying and alone except for its passive witness.

He closed the shutters and took a last walk down to the café. The street was now washed and scrubbed and had a slight smell of chlorine. At the café he ordered a coffee and a Metaxa and sat watching the familiar scene. Perhaps it was time to go home.

Chapter 30

He got back from the conference to a stream of requests, appointments, and meetings and it was hard to hang onto the peace of the holiday, his walks by the sea and meals lingered over. One good thing was that he was seeing Renée in the afternoon. Ali was scratchy, behaviour he recognised from old whenever he went away, Barry was distracted and yet nothing had really changed.

He rang the doorbell and heard the familiar tinkling somewhere deep in the house. When Renée opened the door, they hugged briefly. He was aware of her warm bosom pressing gently against him, the softness and strength of the ample body, a comfort that causes a momentarily feeling of tearfulness.

'You look well,' she said leading the way. He noticed her slow gait and the heaviness in her walk as if he were seeing it for the first time. Strands of hair escaped from her bun and curled round her neck in little grey ringlets.

They didn't say much at first and sat in a comfortable silence. The familiar room with the Persian carpet and Renée sitting in her high-backed wicker chair, her feet resting on the blue foot-rest gave a reassuring sense of peace. Around the walls framed pictures covered the walls. Scenes from her native Germany and on a shelf, gifts from grateful patients and with them, the small alabaster horse, he'd brought her from a previous Greek holiday.

'It's been a while,' said Renée eventually. 'Was it long enough?'

'It will do,' he said, 'Before I went I felt wrung out, I could hardly hang onto the bit left that is me, like a piece of meat that's being consumed by maggots. I feared that in the end, all that would be left would be a small pool of liquid.' Kitchen noises could be heard from the interior of the house.

He shut the door quietly behind him. Drizzle was falling and light from the street-lamp glistened in the puddles. He thought of Renée going to the kitchen, eating the supper that Arnold had prepared, and watching a programme on the television or reading. It was a nice picture, but to enjoy that you needed someone who was a real companion and he wasn't sure if he was ready to settle for that yet. His step quickened and he felt grateful to Renée for giving him the space to think about the possibilities ahead.

Chapter 31

It was a very different Brenda who walked into Ash's room nine months later. He hardly recognised her. She was thinner and her hair was shorter and she seemed subdued.

'What do you think?' Barry had asked a few weeks before. 'Has it been long enough? She's had a tough time.'

'How long since she's been out?'

'Six months.'

'Is she working?'

'No – she's no way ready. She's physically and emotionally frail still. She really wants to join a group here ... I saw her last week. I think she's made a good enough separation and I want to consider her wish to come here, but I wanted to know what you think.' Ash was finding it hard to concentrate but was aware that Barry was more approachable. Maybe the row had helped.

'What would be against offering her a place?' Ash said, 'She's known, I suppose.'

'I've thought about that but none of the new patients in the group would be known to her, I checked, but obviously she would know Rosemary. That might be a problem.'

'I'm interested that you're considering it,' Ash said.

'So am I. It's just, when I met her last week, she was like a puppy that's been kicked. I found myself wanting, to help her. She still wants to be in your group and I couldn't really see what's wrong with that. She won't ever work here again. She nearly died, you know. It's changed her. She has little family support, just a sister ... and I don't know what else to suggest. The Fairlawn's group is finishing in the autumn and it would be a long wait till a new group starts. Mia's taking her sabbatical and all her patients have taken up the spare places – but it's not really about that. I want to help her.'

You're getting soft, old buddy, Ash thought but it seemed there was something about Brenda that was even affecting him.

Chapter 32

What's this about Brenda Chit? The bloody woman's coming back. Can't we ever get shot of her?' Ali shoved a pile of papers to one side and perched on his desk. Ash wished she wouldn't. It was both irritating and distracting. 'Petri's agreed to her joining a group. Is he off his head?'

'I've agreed to it too,' Ash said. 'She's going to join my Thursday group.'

'What! Are you both nuts? You know what she's like, and she knows stuff, and … she'll know the patients.'

'No she won't. We've checked. Anyway, what stuff Ali?' Ash asked deliberately.

'You know, records and …'

'And?' Ash looked into the bright hazel eyes, the whites surprisingly clear. 'And?' he repeated. He didn't want to get into this now but it was time that she knew he knew about the complaint. They'd hedged round it for too long. 'What is it about her coming back that concerns you so much? She's been very ill. She's not the same and she'll never work here again.'

'I know that, but unless she's had a ruddy lobotomy she'll still know things.'

'What things? What is it about her? Look, I've agreed to her joining my group so she is coming back – it will happen.' Ali frowned. He could almost tell what she was thinking. With Brenda gone, she could put the problem behind her. At moments like this, when she was vulnerable he found her especially attractive. He knew though, that tempted as he sometimes was, she would be lethal for him. Together they would roll into a drunken, crazy life only pulling themselves together for work until one day, it and they would fall apart. He was very fond of her and her continual seduction was difficult to resist but it was essential that he did. Ali was looking down swinging her foot.

'Can we go for a drink tonight?' she said. Ash looked quizzical. 'I'd like to talk.'

'About this?' he asked. Ali shot him a look.

'Among other things,' she said tersely.
'OK. I'm finished at five.'
'Right. Let's go into town. Away from this place.'

Chapter 33

A new group member

Somebody new was joining the group in a couple of weeks. Ash had told her just as they were preparing to go into the session and that he would tell her a bit more after the group. He'd been in a meeting that morning and there hadn't been much time to catch up. Leila was interested. Like a new baby in the family, her supervisor had once said. She could imagine that the group would have feelings about it. She hoped Ash's attention would not be too distracted by this new person, and there seemed to be something about this woman, Brenda, she thought she was called.

She followed Ash down the stairs. His hair was thinning on the top, she noticed. They had a couple of minutes to go and he walked slowly, sliding his hand along the banister. Had her sister had feelings about her when she was born? She would have been four. Tanya was just her lovely sister, always kind, and who she could always talk to. It wasn't the same with her brother.

Her mother seemed to be pregnant for ages with him and sometimes stayed in bed for days at a time. Once her mother showed Leila her enormous tummy, laughing at her and kissing her when she said she didn't like it, didn't like the skin stretched and laced with blue veins. When the baby was born, he never stopped crying. She couldn't like him. Tanya was so patient with him but she wished she would dislike him as she did. It felt as if something had come between them.

She was pleased to see that all the group were there. Ash closed the door behind her. She waited for him to take his seat and then took the only other seat which was next to him. It felt a bit close. This first bit, when often the group was silent, was still difficult for her, but she was learning to bear the discomfort and today took the time to look around and try to gauge how they were feeling. Norma was looking around eagerly and gave her a smile as she caught her eye. Both Carl and Steph were looking at the floor and Peter was red-faced and sweaty as usual.

The flowers on the table were especially lovely this morning, like a painting, and Ash had put two sprigs of rosemary with them and a yellow rose that was just opening. She thought she could smell the rosemary. She never saw him arrange the flowers but guessed he did it when he arrived. Ronnie was staring out of the window and April was picking at her nail varnish. Leila looked awkwardly at Ash. From the side, he looked a bit stern though she saw that he too was observing the group. Unusually he was the first to speak.

'I need to tell you that there will be a new person joining the group the week after next,' he said. Nobody said anything but they were all looking at him.

'That's good,' said Norma. Steph scowled at her.

'Is it a man or a woman?' Ronnie asked.

'A woman,' said Ash.

'Does she have a name?' Norma asked. Ash smiled at her.

'You can ask her, Norma.'

'Oh, yes,' Norma said. There was a silence then Ronnie turned to her.

'Have you met her, Leila?' She felt put on the spot. She looked at Ash, who gave a shrug but she saw he was smiling. She decided on the truth.

'No, Ronnie,' she said, 'she will be as new to me as you.' Ronnie seemed satisfied with that.

Leila looked at the clock. There was about ten minutes left of the session.

Steph said, 'This new person who's coming … I thought the group was full.' Ash looked at her. 'I mean we've only just got used to each other, haven't we?' She looked round but nobody met her eye.

'It sounds as if you've got some feelings about it?' Ash said.

'No, well, maybe.'

'What feelings?'

'Well, like I said, we're just getting used to each other.'

'You.'

'You what?'

'You … you are just getting used to everybody.'

'Yea, but I expect everybody feels the same.'

'How do you know? You could check?' Ash said.

'Yes, well, do you?' she addressed the group.

'I like the idea of somebody new,' said Norma.

'You would …' Steph was quelled by a look from Ash.

'I'll like her if she's pretty,' said Carl. The group laughed a little uneasily. Linda was staring at him.

'You've said that to me before. Is that all that matters?' she said. Carl blushed.

'No, you are pretty but … I mean?'

'What do you mean?' said Steph.

'What if she's not pretty?' said Norma. 'Does that mean you won't like her?'

'No, not really … it's just …' Carl looked uncomfortable.

'Does it matter to you?' said Ash, addressing Steph.

'What whether she's pretty?' She made a face.

'No,' said Ash. 'Does it matter to you what somebody looks like? If it was a man joining, for instance?'

'Haven't given it any thought,' she said.

'I think it matters. I think it matters a lot,' said April. 'Everybody judges by appearance. It's horrible if you're not pretty.' The group fell silent again.

'It sounds as if some of you might have feelings about the new person even before you've met her,' Leila said boldly.

'Not really,' said Norma, 'we just wondered what she is like.'

'You wondered?' said Ash.

'Yes, I wondered, but no, I don't really. I don't mind what she looks like.'

'I think I do,' said Carl.

'That's because you're a perv,' said Steph.

'Really Steph,' said Norma. 'You can't say things like that to Carl. You know what he means.'

'Why not? For all I know he's looking at me and I don't know what he's thinking.'

'I'm not, Steph,' Carl said, sitting forward. 'I think you're pretty too. I don't understand, aren't I supposed to say it?'

Leila looked at Ash. There was a pause.

'There seem to be two things,' said Ash.

'Here we go – the explanation,' said Steph, sitting back in her chair. Ash looked at her quizzically.

'Well, I mean,' said Steph, 'Carl is saying the he judges people by how they look and if they're not pretty he won't like them and that makes me feel uncomfortable, and now I suppose you're going to explain why it isn't really like that and we should all try and understand it.'

'You seem angry,' said Ash. 'Who are you angry with?'

'You, no Carl. No, I don't know. I just hate the way people make judgements all the time.'

'Do you?' he asked.

'No, I don't.'

'Yes, you do,' said April. 'The other week you said Norma could have her hair cut in a more modern way. If appearances aren't important, how does that make sense?'

'That's different,' said Steph.

'What would you think if somebody walked in now, what would you think about them?' April said.

'I'd be open-minded.' Leila heard a snigger. 'I would,' she said.

'If we go back to Carl,' said Ash, 'you might like to check out with him what he meant. I heard him say, he would like the new person if she was pretty. Is that right Carl?' Carl nodded. 'And Steph, you say you don't mind what somebody looks like and April says she thinks people judge by appearances. So, what can we make of these different views?' The group looked thoughtful.

Steph was staring at April. 'I suppose I do care, a bit.' They all turned to her. 'It was what you said about somebody coming in now. If say they were fat or dirty- looking or frightening, I guess I would have an opinion. I mean you can't help it, can you?'

'I wouldn't mind if she was fat,' said Carl. 'As long as ...' Steph mimicked, '... she was pretty.'

'Yes,' said Carl. 'I still don't get it. Why can't I say if someone is pretty,' He was looking at Ash.

'You could ask the group,' said Ash. Carl looked round. Nobody seemed to want to answer, then Ronnie said,

'I don't think it's that you can't say it. I notice how people look. I try not to but I do, it's just ... I don't know. Maybe if, say, it was a man joining the group and, say, Steph said she would like him if he was handsome. What would you think?' Carl looked thoughtful.

'Um ... I suppose I would wonder if she thought I was handsome and as I'm not, I would feel she would like the new person more than me.'

'Exactly,' said Peter.

'But that isn't what I mean and even if it was, just because I don't say it, I still think it. Am I supposed to lie then?'

'Has this been a problem before, Carl?' Ash asked.

'At Coleman's I got into trouble with the woman at the next desk and was asked to leave.'

'What happened?' asked Steph.

'I said she had nice legs and she complained that I was sexually harassing her, but she did have nice legs,' he added. Ronnie leaned forward.

'It's not really about whether she had nice legs or not, Carl. You just shouldn't say it?'

'Why?'

'Because it makes the person feel uncomfortable. What if I said something about you? Like I think you've got a big nose or something.'

'But I haven't,' said Carl.

'I know but if you had.'

'But I haven't ...'

'Carl! Dr Jones, explain to him,' said Steph in exasperation.

'You want me to explain, Steph. You all seem to be doing fine by yourselves. But I am aware that we are nearly out of time.' They looked surprised. 'It does seem though that whatever we feel about it, we do all make judgements about each other but why we do that, might be more to do with us. So, something to think about and perhaps this is a good place to finish.'

Ash stood up. Leila stood too and followed him out. As they went up the stairs, she noticed that none of the group had left the room.

Chapter 34

It was strange going back. Brenda hesitated by one of the pillars, not sure if she could go in. It all looked the same, Dr Jones's Saab was there, but seeing Rosemary's bicycle gave her a jolt. It would be difficult seeing her but then things were different now. Now she was a patient and she knew it. She needed to see Dr Jones. He would protect her, be her buoy in this flat sea. The breeze tugged at her skirt and, picking up a crisp packet, sent it in a whirlwind near her feet. Almost imperceptible, she felt a hand at her back, gently propelling her towards the door.

Through the glass door, she saw the broken umbrella still under the bench. There was nobody at the reception desk. She pushed open the door and turned left down the corridor and into the toilet, locking the door. She took time to wash her hands and then slide the bolt back quietly. There was still nobody about so she went into the kitchen. The door of the group room was shut. She looked at her watch. It was ten to ten. She heard a door open and footsteps. Whoever it was went into the toilet.

Seeing him, sitting opposite, reassured her. The same kindly face, the solid frame, the comfyness of his appearance, the rightness of him. He'd smiled and welcomed her. It was surely a special smile of recognition. When he interviewed her last week, there had been so much she wanted to say. She felt calm but that was probably the medication. She just didn't get upset in the same way now, everything was flatter.

The room was warm. Some of the plants had been replaced, she noticed, and there were new blue chairs. He wore the same navy sleeveless jumper and had a neatly ironed shirt. Who'd ironed it? she thought, and then stopped herself. She would not think about that.

She'd looked at the others as they arrived, but then kept her eyes down. She recognised the one called Leila from the ward round. That made her feel a bit sick. How close was she to Dr Jones? There were six of them. Three men.

There'd been groups at the hospital. She'd tried to be interested but she never liked the other patients to begin with, though one or two turned out to be OK. She still wished she'd been able to have individual therapy with him, but she had to take what was offered. She'd learned that.

The tall dull-looking woman, who said her name was Norma, had asked her name, straight away. She'd hoped nobody would ask her anything more and they hadn't. Too polite perhaps or maybe they'd been told not to. In some of the hospital groups, you were expected to do things, answer questions about your feelings and do homework. Couldn't see the point really but sometimes it was interesting. She'd asked if this group was like that and Dr Jones had said, no. The woman Steph hadn't even said hello and looked angry. Brenda sensed animosity. She was quite attractive. Did Dr Jones think so? The older man, Ronnie, seemed OK.

Steph turned to her. 'Have you been in a group before?' she asked.

'Yes,' said Brenda.

'Where?' Steph asked. Brenda looked at Dr Jones.

'Maybe Brenda doesn't want to say yet. It must be hard to come into a group like this,' Norma said. Brenda felt a wave of gratitude. Steph shrugged.

'I was just asking,' she said. It was funny, Brenda thought, like a game. She knew Dr Jones and the woman Leila knew about her, but they wouldn't say, she guessed. But she knew they knew.

'It's the way you ask it, Steph,' said Norma. Brenda was surprised at her boldness. She didn't look like she would hurt a fly. After that nobody asked her anything more.

Norma seemed to have been in some sort of place where people lived together. The man Carl, looked at her when he wasn't looking at the floor. Linda looked like she was about to collapse and didn't really say anything. Ronnie did most of the talking. He was a grandfather, she was surprised to learn, but he lived by himself. Was he widowed? At first he seemed kind and normal and she couldn't see why he was here, but after the initial interest, he seemed to withdraw, and stared out of the window a lot.

For a while she was pleased to be left alone but then she began to be irritated. It was like she wasn't here. She saw Norma looking at her.

'I was wondering how you were feeling?' she asked.

'OK,' Brenda managed. Steph looked away dismissively.

'Would you like to say something about yourself, Brenda?' said Dr Jones. Oh that kindly tone. So understanding. 'Or would you rather say it in your own time?' She felt they were all looking at her.

'OK,' she said. There was nothing to lose anymore. She'd been stripped of all pride and dignity over the last months. This was just another group, what did it matter if they knew? The important person was Dr Jones and he knew already. Probably he would like her to say something.

'I was in hospital until six months ago,' she said. 'I tried to kill myself.' There was a silence. She dared a glance round. Nobody seemed too shocked, in fact, they looked interested and well, sympathetic. 'I haven't been working since then.'

'I haven't worked for ten years,' said Ronnie.

'Did something happen?' asked Steph.

'I took an overdose once,' said Carl. 'I was in hospital too.' She caught Linda looking at her but she lowered her eyes quickly.

'I'm glad you told us,' said Norma and it sounded sincere, like she really was. Brenda looked at Dr Jones. He gave her an encouraging smile. He was pleased with her. Maybe she was doing it right. She reached up as a feeling like a feather brushed against her cheek. She could be a model patient, build on that special bond.

Chapter 35

Ash was determined to drive. He didn't trust Ali's driving, let alone if she was going to drink. She directed him to a wine bar not far from the centre of the town He picked her up from her flat which meant he had time to change, and they wouldn't leave work together. Somehow it always got noticed.

Ali greeted the barman and within minutes a bottle and glasses were on the table. They were the usual huge winebar glasses, no single units here. He stopped her filling his glass and diluted his with water. Ali's first glass disappeared almost before he had taken a sip. He hated having to notice this. In the past an evening with Ali meant a hangover but while it was happening it was good. Now it was different. Now he knew there was a cost. Perhaps that was what she was going to talk about. In spite of this, he began to relax. He liked being with her. He liked the way heads turned and she was amusing and quick. The wine bar was filling up. He liked that too. The Friday night crowd, relaxing after a hard week.

Ali filled his glass even though it wasn't empty and filled her own. She leaned towards him a lot and he loved the way her hair swung forward then settled right back into place when she sat back or shook her head. Perhaps this was OK. He took another drink. and this time he didn't dilute it. They finished the bottle and Ali went out for a cigarette. She returned with another bottle, banging it down on the table. She smelt slightly of cigarettes.

'Tell me about the Chit woman,' she said filling her glass. 'Why have you agreed to it?'

'Because I think she should come back,' he said.

'Why?' Ali looked perplexed. 'She's trouble.'

'Not for me, she's not. A bit highly strung perhaps,' he said, then laughed. 'I haven't used that expression for years. I'm highly strung,' he repeated and laughed again. Ali was looking at him, amused but frowning.

'What's got into you? What you laughing about?'

'That phrase. It's the sort of thing my mother ... Barbara would have said.' He found himself smiling idiotically at the memory.

'But what about that incident? She was pretty aggressive.'

'Yes, but she's been ill and in hospital since then. She's changed. She did well and I think we can help continue the process. She's not a bad person Ali.' Ali looked thoughtful. 'What is it? Why are you so worried?'

'She will be trouble,' she said.

'Yes, so you've said but I don't know what you mean.' Ash felt the lie expedient.

'You know she threatened to put in a complaint about me?' she said.

'Did she do it?' Ash asked.

'Well, no, she got carted off, but aren't you interested in what it was about?'

'If you want to tell me.'

'Oh come on Ash. Cut the bullshit. You know don't you.'

'Actually Ali, I don't really know. I knew there was something. Why don't you tell me?'

'I caught her listening outside the group room.' This he hadn't heard before.

'What do you mean?'

'You were taking a group and there she was ear glued to the door. When I confronted her, she said she was worried about you because Barry was boasting he had a knife.' Ash was digesting this news. They drank in silence for a while. Ali refilled her glass and he put his hand over his.

'So what's this got to do with the complaint?'

'Well, when I confronted her and said I should report her, she said to watch out because she could report me.' She took another swig. 'She couldn't of course, but it worried me.'

'Why?'

'Why did it worry me? Because even when you know there's no grounds, it's disturbing. Come on, you know that.' Ash nodded.

The noise of the bar had increased but he'd hardly noticed it until now. The wine was making him feel mellow and the familiar sense of well-being was developing. What Ali did with her life was her business. He suddenly couldn't be bothered. He wanted to talk about other things. To laugh and enjoy her company. He uncrossed his legs and accidentally brushing against her foot. Could they? Ali didn't seem to notice.

'She could still make trouble,' she said. Ash was sorry that she was not going to let it drop.

'OK, Ali. What do you think she could complain about? She's not one of your patients. I didn't know you had anything to do with her.' Ali let out a sigh and looked directly at him.

'She knows somebody who works in Strakers. He told me once when I was in there. Said he knew her. I go in there sometimes at lunch time and one day, I'd had a bit more than usual to drink and I was putting my head down on my desk and she came in. It was nothing ... it was only once but after that I felt she was watching me.' Ash didn't say anything. It wasn't necessary. At least now she wasn't in complete denial.

She drained the bottle and leaning back in her chair, her conversation turned to other things and other people,

'Come on,' she said suddenly, 'let's go. This place is getting crowded. Let's find somewhere else.

It was drizzling as they left the bar. Ali put her coat over her head then reached for his hand. They ran along the pavement, she pulling him and he laughing and trying to keep up. It felt good. He hadn't run like this for years. In the car they sank into the seats laughing and catching their breath. Ali shook her coat, flung it on the back seat and then leaned back against the door, half facing him.

'You haven't said anything. I want to know what you think.'

'About what?' he said. This was a pity. He thought they'd done with that. She reached in her bag for a cigarette but catching his eye, put them back again, then hesitated.

'If I open the window?' she said. He shook his head and she put them away.

'You can see why I'm worried about her coming back and I'm still surprised you're in favour of it.' Reluctantly he realised it was not to be avoided. Her skirt had ridden up and from this angle it was hard not to let his eyes wander.

'What is it you think she is going to say?' he said.

'I suppose that I sometimes have a drink at lunch time.'

'Do you?'

'Is the Pope catholic?' she said then went serious. 'You know I do, but I can handle it. It's never affected the patients.'

'Do you ever worry that it might?'

'It won't,' she said. 'I'm not sparked out. It's just a couple of gins … sometimes.'

'So why are you worried … if you can handle it?'

'That's a funny tone. What are you saying?'

'I'm not saying anything Ali. This is your business but because you're so concerned, I'm wondering if you are worried?'

'I'm not one of your bloody patients,' she said pulling her legs back and sitting round to face the front.

'Look. I like a drink. We both do. I have one in the day to relax me. It doesn't hurt anyone. You'd think I was a bloody alchi.' The silence weighed heavily. Suddenly she sat up straight. 'Come on. Let's go. I've got some champagne at home.'

He drove carefully, aware that he had had a drink. He had to take her home, he told himself later. When she invited him in, it was not difficult to say yes. This wasn't the first time they'd ended up at one or other of their flats and once she stayed over, sleeping on his sofa, completely out of it. Somehow though he didn't feel totally easy about it tonight, but he could do with some strong coffee and he could take a taxi home. It wasn't far.

He waited while she opened the door. Everything in the flat was immaculate. Large windows overlooked the park. The pale settee and table were almost the only furniture except for neat shelves. A stove gave a warm glow, and on the floor by the window stood a large vase of flowers: tall, curled, spiky and clearly expensive. Strangely it didn't smell of cigarettes.

Ali went quickly to the window and let down two of the blinds leaving the centre one up so that the lights of the town could be seen. She disappeared into the kitchen and he sank onto the sofa. Soon she appeared with a tray with coffee, glasses, a bottle of champagne, her cigarettes and black and white lighter. She had taken off her jacket. Her slim arms had the same pale skin as her face. She opened the champagne expertly and he didn't resist when she poured out two glasses. The fire flickered, the room was warm and comfortable, what was wrong with a bit more to drink?

Ali crossed to the window and lowered the last blind. Then she came and sat next to him. Very next to him. As she sat she put her hand on his leg, to steady herself? They clinked glassed and she leaned back. This time there was no mistaking the closeness. It was clear that she was interested and he certainly was. It was only good sense that was making him resist, all his instincts told him to go for it. He wriggled so that there was a bit of space between them, and then regretted it. They drank silently. It was good champagne. Ali certainly knew her wine. Leaning forward she reached for her cigarettes, putting her hand rather higher on his leg as she did so. She leaned back smiling impishly. It was too much. His resistance was going.

She smoked and filled their glasses again. Then stubbing out her cigarette, she took a drink and turned to face him, drawing up her knees. Then she leaned towards him, pulling him towards her. Pushing closer her hand reached down and as it touched him, all sense left him. Her mouth was warm and biting. He felt her tugging at his shirt. Pulling at his tie. She seemed to have slipped almost under him, the pleasure was excruciating.

The phone rang next to the sofa. They jumped.

'Don't worry about it,' Ali said, pulling at his belt, but it was enough. Sudden clarity came to him. What the hell was he doing? She was a colleague. He had to work with her. What about Eva? He pulled away, fumbling with his shirt and standing up. The top of one of her stockings was showing. Longing shot through him again.

'What's wrong?' said Ali looking surprised.

'I can't Ali. It won't do. I'm sorry. I shouldn't have come back.' His one thought now was to get out and to get home. Fumbling, mumbling he walked towards the door, aware of Ali's look of anger and hurt.

'It's not you,' he said. 'There's nothing I would like more. I just can't.' He thought he saw tears as he grabbed his coat. He ran down the stairs to the street.

He couldn't drive. He'd have to leave his car. All he wanted was to get home. He began to walk quickly.

In fifteen minutes he let himself into his flat. His head was beginning to ache and his mind was swimming. What had he done and could it be repaired?

The alarm woke him. His head and genitals ached and he had an erection reminiscent of adolescence. He felt guilty and depressed and he chided himself for his stupidity. He took a shower, had two cups of strong black coffee, and, feeling slightly better, left the flat.
Repeating last night's walk, he returned to his car. Looking up he saw thankfully that the blinds of Ali's flat were still down. It would be awkward bumping into her, but he felt sad too. It felt as if something had been spoiled.

Chapter 36

Brenda had asked to have a one-to-one session with him. He wasn't quite sure why, as she seemed to be getting on well in the group. Apart from Steph, she seemed friendly with the others and joined in. She'd put on a bit of weight and it suited her and she'd done something to her hair. He wasn't sure what. He'd found himself staring one week, trying to work out what it was. Perhaps the colour was different. She'd noticed him staring and he'd smiled and looked away quickly. He often caught her looking at him and, though he tried to encourage her to speak to the whole group, most of her conversation was directed to him.

He didn't usually encourage one-to-ones, telling them to bring it back to the group, but this was the second time she'd asked and ... well, he'd agreed. She knocked quietly and shut the door carefully behind her before taking the seat opposite him. This was very different from the way she'd barged about when she worked here. She had never mentioned this connection in the group and he had not thought it helpful to refer to it. The only person who really knew her and who she might come across was Rosemary, but whether by accident or design, Rosemary worked at Fairlawn's on a Thursday.

'You wanted to speak to me, Brenda. Are you sure you couldn't bring whatever it is to the group?' Brenda stared at him and then shook her head. He waited.

'I couldn't say it in the group. It wouldn't be fair.' she said.

'What wouldn't be fair?' he asked.

'My dream,' she said.

'Dreams are perfectly acceptable to talk about in the group,' he said.

'Not this one,' she said and looked down.

'I don't suppose people would be shocked, whatever it was.'

'They would by this one and anyway, it's not for them.' He was beginning to feel irritated. It had been a mistake to see her by herself. This could perfectly well have been brought to the group and would have done her more good. His mind drifted to Ali again. There was still a slight ache. Rationally he was glad he'd resisted but what pleasure had he denied himself?

'It's about you,' Brenda said, 'and me.' He felt his heart quicken and the beginnings of a different unease.

'About us?' he asked. 'I don't understand.'

'It's not easy to talk about it,' she said. 'I know you know … but it still isn't easy.'

'Know what?' he asked.

'About us,' she said.

'What about us, Brenda? I don't understand.' Dawning though was some uncomfortable realisation of what it might be about.

'In my dream we were … you know.' Her eyes were large and soft, looking at him.

'A dream is not real, Brenda … maybe you'd better just tell me about it and we can see what it might mean.'

'But it is real. Yes, it's a dream but it's what I want.' Colour had slowly crept up her neck and to her face. 'I think about you all the time, Dr Jones. I think you feel the same and I know you can't show it in front of the others but …'

'Brenda. Sometimes we dream about things we would like to happen but they may not be literal or true.'

'This is,' she interrupted. He needed time to think. He remembered Ali's story about finding her outside the door and the misunderstanding about her joining his group when she worked here. It was beginning to make sense now. 'I dream about us meeting when you've finished work and going and having a meal together and …' Brenda said.

'Brenda. I can hear that you have become very preoccupied with me and I understand that, and that is OK. You also know that nothing can come of it. It is all right to have fantasies but nothing is going to happen.'

'I know. I know you can't do anything now. It wouldn't be fair on the others, but I can wait.' They sat in silence for a while, and then Ash said,

'Have you thought about why you might be feeling like this about me?'

'Apart from because you're lovely and kind?' she said flirtatiously. Ash looked serious.

'Sometimes people in a group look at the therapist as a sort of parent. You might see me as a father.'

'No way. My father was a bully.'

'Exactly, Brenda. You might imagine that I would be a better father and so you have warm feelings towards me.'

'You would be, I'm sure about that but that's not why I feel like I do about you. These are not childish feelings,' she said lowering her eyes and looking up at him.

'I know that's how it feels at the moment Brenda, and it's not unusual for patients to think they have fallen in love with their therapists.'

'So, I'm just like everybody else. I don't think so.' The tone was sharp, more like the old Brenda.

'Brenda. You could bring this to the group you know. We can work with it.'

'You must be joking. How could I say this in the group?'

'Just like you've said it to me today.'

'I couldn't and I wouldn't want to. It's between us. It's private.'

'There is nothing wrong with having these feelings,' he said gently, 'but they probably belong to other people and other times and besides, if you don't bring them to the group, you will be stuck with them. I cannot see you on your own again but I want to help you understand and work with the feelings that at the moment seem to relate to me. Does that make sense?' Brenda looked sulky.

'They won't change. I know it's true and I understand that you can't admit it but I can't talk about it in the group. I just can't,' she said.

'OK I hear that is how it seems at the moment, but try and keep an open mind. We need to finish now but I will see you on Thursday. Good bye.'

Brenda got up. She gave him a last lingering look and left the room. Ash sighed. He put his head back and breathed deeply. How bizarre was that? First the business with Ali, now Brenda. What was going on? His headache was getting worse and he longed above all to be at home and in bed – alone.

Chapter 37

Ash decided that this evening he would walk to Renée's. That is, he would drive most of the way and walk the last half-mile. The trees were just changing colour and the walk through the village would be pleasant. He parked the car and took out his coat. It was the first time he had felt the need for a coat this year. In the distance a tractor was spraying slurry and the gulls followed, diving and calling, their cries so evocative of his summer.

He turned right at the crossroads and along the path to the stream. Red hawthorn berries glistened in the hedges. He couldn't remember whether they were hips or haws, but the thought made him smile. Strings of blackberries hung amongst the leaves and he stopped and picked some. The fields had been ploughed into rich brown furrows and in the distance he could see a farm and some cottages. Smoke curled from a chimney, and although it was not yet dark, some windows were lit. It looked idyllic, real homes, real people, legitimately tired after a hard day's work. He walked on up the lane. Why should they be any more or less happy and fulfilled than anyone else? No doubt their life had its difficulties and worries like anybody else. He was painting a romantic picture.

The canopy of trees opened up and in a field, near an oak tree, he saw six chestnut foals, the scene like a Stubbs painting. He stopped, captivated. This was truly beautiful. A noise startled the foals and they ran for a moment then stopped, then were off again, kicking up their heels, putting their heads down, their mothers looking up, then returning to their grazing.

At the end of the village, he clicked open Renée's gate and walked up the path. Already Arnold had dug over the vegetable patch and tidied up the remaining plants. He bent to avoid a wisteria branch, and pressed the bell.

After half an hour, he hadn't addressed the business of Brenda. It wasn't just Brenda, it was the whole thing, Ali and well – all of it. What he needed to talk about, openly and frankly, was sex, his own needs, his fantasies, but this was supervision, not therapy. After a pause he said, 'I've got a patient in my new group who's got a bit fixated on me. I didn't realise the extent of it. In fact I hadn't picked it up at all. I must be slipping.'

'Who is it?' Renée asked.

'The new woman, Brenda, I think I've talked about her before. She was the one who got so upset when she couldn't be in a group at 'The Firs'.'

'In your group, if I remember correctly,' said Renée.

'Yes, my group.'

'So how does she show up in your group now? No, don't worry if it isn't important. It's just erotic transference … isn't that what you are saying.'

'Yes,' he said, but he didn't want to continue. He felt irritated that Renée, usually so sensitive, was simply giving it a name as if the difficulties were nothing. How often did it happen to her? he thought savagely, and then caught his breath. Hadn't he only the other week, felt a tear when they hugged?

'Is she an individual patient?' Renée asked.

'No thank God, but before I realised this was happening, I saw her on her own.' Renée raised her eyebrows. 'She'd asked twice. I thought it was something personal she wanted to tell me.'

'It was,' Renée said.

'Yes, true,' he managed a half smile. 'I can usually cope with it … mind you it's a while since it's happened.'

'That you know about,' said Renée.

'Yes, of course. It's always around.' Why was she being so unhelpful? Now she was almost joking about it. He sat quietly.

'Have I offended you?'

'No … no, not really.'

'Not really?'

'Well, OK you seem to be making light of it, and I'm struggling a bit.'

'I'm sorry. I didn't realise you were so worried. Let's think more seriously about it.' She paused 'It is important that she is able to explore her feelings, whatever they are. That's the theory anyway.'

Ash nodded. 'It is really only a problem if our needs are not sufficiently resolved. So, where are you with this?'

'You always know, don't you?' he said.

'It's my job to know and anyway it's easy for me, I'm not the one who is having the feelings. I am imagining that you are not having erotic feelings towards this ... Brenda, isn't it?'

'No, not at all, but she does generate strong feelings. The few dealings I've had with her in the past, have always left me feeling incompetent and on edge.'

'And you were unaware of her feeling towards you?'

'Totally. I certainly dismissed them if I did notice, though Alison said something once, but it didn't really register. So much was going on.' He felt uncomfortable at the mention of Ali.

'Of course it's more difficult to work with this in a group – but very rich if you can. Clearly you can't see her individually now this has come up. Are you concerned about how to work with this or concerned that you might not remain professional?'

'I'm not worried about staying professional. No that's not it. 'It's ...' he stopped, trying to think what it was that was difficult. Could he say what he was thinking? It might be easier if Renée was a man. 'I think my concern is that the sexual projections will affect me, not that I fear I will act out, simply, well, there hasn't been much recently and this highlights it.'

'At last. Now we're getting to it. When are you seeing Eva next?' Ash laughed at the directness.

'Not till the new year.'

'Could you go and see her? Take a week-end off?'

'I could, but this is a bit prescriptive. Go and get my rocks off for the week-end, and it won't be a problem.' Renée said nothing.

'Are there other temptations around?' Ash half gasped. Had she seen his discomfort?

'Well, there's always temptation. I'm not blind or that old yet.' Renée raised her eyebrows. 'I notice women, of course. Like on holiday. It's hard not to. It's so in your face but I notice people in general. I might look at ... anybody who is interesting.' Renée pursed her lips.

'*Mein freund, das ist bunkum,*' she said and they laughed.

'OK. What am I saying? I like women, occasionally get frustrated or turned on, but not in a way that is a problem. I am a bit preoccupied with sex in general at this stage in my life, and what I want to do about it, and just at the moment, it is being offered from unsuitable sources.'

'I take it you don't mean Brenda.'

'No, no, not Brenda. Fortunately I don't find her attractive.'

'But there is someone you do?'

And Ash told her. The near miss with Ali. The bizarreness of all this happening now. How it was leaving him sad and bewildered. How he didn't worry that he would act out, but it was disturbing him. And there it was, out.

'And Brenda? Do you think you can help her work with it in the group?'

'I can try. It's already in the air. She may not be able to help it.'

'It will cause a lot of feeling.'

'It will.'

'Are the group up to it, do you think?'

'I'm not sure. Anyway, I will just have to see, but thanks.'

Returning to his car, he breathed in the crisp air and realised that he felt lighter. He stepped onto the verge to allow a tractor to pass. The second time he'd been on the verge this week, he thought. The driver, ruddy-faced and flat-capped, waved a thank you and the timeless image made things feel right with the world. He walked with a brisk step back through the village to his car, aware still of some sadness when he thought about Ali.

Chapter 38

April

April lay back and took her arms out from under the duvet. The light was just visible through the curtain which meant it was later than she thought. She hadn't heard the neighbours leaving, so she must have fallen asleep in the early hours. Her aunt would be long gone.

She felt awful. The same lead weight around her heart. On a scale of ten, how was she today? Two, maybe three. Perhaps this time the depression was not going to lift. She felt small relief in the thought that if it got much worse, she could put an end to it.

She smelled.

She pulled the duvet up under her chin so she couldn't smell herself. The room was shadowy. If she didn't look at the clock she couldn't know the time, so she needn't feel guilty. Guilty for being a slob who couldn't get up in the morning. Who, apart from to PISS AND SHIT she hadn't meant to shout, would stay in bed all day.

So what – who did it hurt? Good people, together people, they got up early, hoovered the house before they went to work. Took the children to school. Made their husband's sandwiches. Bollocks. Bollocks.

She buried her head under the duvet but then she could smell herself again. It wasn't fair. She reached for the alarm clock. Fuck. It was Thursday. Group day. It was ten to nine. She threw the covers back, then sank back. It was too late. She'd never make it even if she rushed. What did it matter if she went? It might be good to make them miss her. They might think about how they'd been with her. Nobody ever asking if she was all right. If she didn't say anything, nobody noticed, except Dr Jones, sometimes. They might wonder why she wasn't there. Norma would worry, but she worried about everyone.

God, the smell again. Had the men she'd been with noticed? They must have done and just not said anything. She lay back, eyes tightly closed. The shame, so familiar, started at her toes, moved through her, gripping and squeezing, taking up residence.

She opened her eyes. She'd like some toast. Eight fifty-five. Five minutes to shower. She looked at the clothes hanging on the chair, trying to make out in the half light what they were. At least she didn't have to be smart for the bloody group. If she did go it would be such a rush. What if the bus was late? She lay back for a minute, then jumped up quickly, crossed the room, half opened the curtain and went into the bathroom.

April compared herself with everybody. That woman was older than her, that one fatter, that one had better hair, that one was smarter, that one looked stupid, that one had the wrong shoes. By the time she got off the bus, April knew she looked a freak and was momentarily surprised when she caught her reflection in the shop window and saw someone almost normal, but then she began picking again. Her hair was awful, her clothes a mess. By the time she turned into Burnham Road, she was Dracula again and even though she'd showered, she could smell herself. How could she go to the group? If she did kill herself, she couldn't do it at night. She smelled so terrible in the morning. Why didn't other people smell?

She'd had her hair cut, last week and when the girl was washing her hair, when she'd had her head back, in the girl's armpit for God's sake, she'd really sniffed, tried to see if she smelled, but there wasn't a trace. How did she do that? She'd been glad when she could leave the hairdresser's. They probably opened the windows when she gone and whispered. She wouldn't go there again.

She knocked on the door, crossing the cavernous space, and took the seat next to Ronnie. There was one empty chair and it took her a minute to work out that it was Brenda who was missing. She'd meant to take her coat off but she couldn't now. If she did they would smell her. She was the last, except for Brenda, but nobody was speaking. Not this again. The bloody silence.

She felt a bit better, seeing the others, but who were they really? They were nothing to her. It wasn't like they were friends. They certainly weren't family. Most of them had family, of a sort. Still nobody said anything. Well, she wasn't going to.

She thought about her mum instead. Norma was a bit like her, except that Norma was thin and not so pretty, no, she was not a bit like her really. She needed her mum now. She might have understood, at least about the depression. It must be inherited. What chance did she have? Well, her mum found a way out.

She shouldn't even think it, but, one thing that was private, that nobody could know, were her thoughts. And it was what she thought. She'd like to get cancer. At least everybody felt sorry for you. They didn't when her mum was depressed but as soon as she got cancer, then it was, 'Oh how terrible' 'You're so brave' and all that. If she had cancer, it would be a legitimate way to die, a way to have some relief.

She looked round almost afraid that somebody might be able to hear her thoughts, and saw that Linda was crying. Leila was looking at her. Didn't look like anybody else had noticed.

'Linda – do you want to say what is upsetting you?' Leila asked. They all looked at Linda. Linda continued to cry. She didn't look up or speak, she just cried. Norma reached for the tissue box and gave it to her. Linda blew her nose but carried on crying. She had on this bobbly pink jumper. It didn't look very clean.

'What's the matter, Linda?' said Carl. 'Why are you sad?' He looked as if he was going to cry too. Linda carried on crying, every so often reaching for a tissue and blowing snottily. Nobody spoke.

'Something is really hurting today, isn't it Linda?' Leila said again. 'Do you want to tell us or would you like to be left alone?' April felt irritated. Why were they giving Linda so much attention? Is that what she should do, cry and cry? Nobody asked her if she was hurting.

Linda was crying louder. It was a bit frightening. Why didn't someone stop her? Now she was sobbing, and beginning to shake. What if she had a fit or something? Suddenly Linda pulled her hearing aids from her ears and slid off the chair onto the floor. Both Leila and Norma went to get up but Dr Jones held up his hand and they sat back down again. Linda lay, curled up crying and hugging her knees while everybody watched.

After about a minute Dr Jones said, 'It looks as if you feel you've hit rock bottom today, Linda. Even the chair can't support you.' The sobbing increased. He nodded to Leila and indicated a cushion on one of the empty chairs. Leila got it and looked questioningly at him. He indicated to Leila to place it under Linda's head. Gently Leila lifted Linda's head and put the cushion under it and then returned to her seat.

'Would you like to stay there for a while?' Dr Jones asked. Linda nodded. The group was silent. April realised that now she didn't feel angry, but sad for Linda. The crying was getting less. After a little while, Linda looked up at Dr Jones, then sat up and put her hearing aids back. She sat for a minute. Dr Jones said,

'I wonder if you feel you could sit back on your chair, Linda?' April held her breath. Linda sat a bit more, then got up and onto the chair, hugging the cushion to herself. She looked up and April found herself smiling at her, as if she'd done something clever.

'How are you feeling now?' Dr Jones said. 'The cushion looks comfortable.' Linda looked at it and then laughed. They all did, with relief. 'So, what has been going on for you, to make you feel so low?' The sad look came back into her face.

'I feel silly now,' she said.

'Do you see anybody here who thinks you are silly?' he said. 'You could take a look around and see.' Linda quickly looked round. 'Well?' he said.

'No, I think everybody looks OK.' The group waited. 'I just want the depression to go away. I thought, after all this time I would feel better, but I don't. Every week I leave feeling flat and tired with the rest of the day ahead.' She took a tissue and blew her nose. 'I want to go home and go to bed but my sister will be there and Wayne and they won't leave me alone if I try and stay in my room. My aunt says I should stand up to them but she isn't there to see what it's like and she doesn't get back from the hospital until late.' She sighed a big sigh. 'Sometimes I go to the Job Centre. Helen, that's the woman I talk to, sometimes has a job for me and I feel excited and I go along to see. They already know I'm deaf but it isn't that. I clam up, and even before they've phoned the Job Centre, I know they're going to say, they're sorry but I wasn't what they were looking for and Helen looks sorry and a bit fed up. I do want to work again. It was just that people frighten me and I don't know how to talk to them.' She had stopped crying now. Her eyes were red and sore looking. April wanted to say something but she didn't know what.

'I think you are disappointed that being in the group has not made you feel any better,' Dr Ash said. April was surprised too. Didn't he mind saying that? It was like he was agreeing the group didn't work.

'I wonder if that is a familiar feeling?' he said. She nodded. 'I bet you are not the only one who knows what disappointment feels like,' he said.

'I get disappointed,' said Peter, 'and I'm depressed.'

'So am I,' said Carl.

'I am too,' April found herself saying. They looked round at each other.

'So that's half of us who are depressed,' said Peter.

'Is this a group for depressives Dr Jones?' Carl said.

Dr. Jones sort of shrugged. 'It seems to be something that a lot of you know about. I wonder if it makes it less frightening … knowing that you are not alone?'

And somehow it did. April felt the most curious thing happening. She felt a surge of warmth towards the group. It was ridiculous. She suddenly wanted to hug somebody. She wouldn't, but it was a nice feeling. She smiled at Linda, who returned the smile. Even Steph was silent and was looking at Linda, a bit puzzled.

After the group ended, April didn't go straight home. She went into BHS and bought a red top from her allowance. She hadn't worn anything bright for ages.

Wayne and her sister were out when she got back, but instead of going to her room, she fried herself an egg and read a magazine. She hoovered the sitting room and tidied up. Then she went to her room.

Chapter 39

The telephone trilled. Ash looked at the clock. Seven fifteen. Who the hell was phoning now? He picked up the phone.

'Ash ...' He recognised Barry Petri's voice. 'Ash – sorry to phone you so early but I thought you'd better know ... one of your patients ... Ronnie Goodly, has OD'd ... It's touch and go. Sorry to wake you with this.'

'Ronnie? Shit,' said Ash. 'When did he do it?'

'Early hours it seems. His sister found him. Called the ambulance but he was pretty far gone when they got to him.' There was a pause. 'They'll want to know when you saw him last ... when did you?'

'Wednesday – no Friday. He was due to have his review on Wednesday but he didn't turn up. Rosemary phoned and gave him another appointment on Friday.'

'How did he seem?'

'OK. A bit low.'

'Is it right that he was in some sort of intelligence work, before the breakdown?'

'Yes, something like that. Look Barry, I can't do this now. I need to think about it. Can I get in touch with the hospital? See how he is?'

'Don't worry. They are going to let me know if there is any news. I'll keep you posted.'

'OK. Thanks. I'll see you later.'

Ash put the phone down. He sat on the edge of the bed. 'Poor bugger,' he thought. Ronnie was just the sort of patient who got overlooked. He felt angry with himself. Another thing he had missed. There really hadn't been any indications. He sighed. How often had he heard that said?

He was cold. He got up and went to the bathroom. He looked awful. Old and crumpled in his striped pyjamas. Geraldine wouldn't have let him wear these. Suddenly he liked them. He did up a button and pulled on his dressing grown. Ronnie. Damn. How dare he do this to him? What if he succeeded? What ever he felt about people's right to die, when it came to it, he didn't mean on his patch.

Chapter 40

The trip down was not a success. It was only sensible for them to travel together but two hours in a car with Geraldine was almost too much for Ash. She criticized his driving and took intakes of breath as he approached roundabouts or negotiated overtaking. It made him nervous, perhaps the desired effect. The timing was inconvenient too, but at the sound of Geraldine's imperious, 'I'm going to visit Tom on Tuesday. I think you should come along too. The psychiatrist is going to talk to us' he'd caved in. Of course he wanted to see Tom, but now there was the enquiry about Ronnie that needed to be done.

The concern was so little about Ronnie, he thought. Everybody rushing around relieved that he hadn't succeeded but worried about how it might look, and little thought given to how Ronnie had felt and the reasons behind it. And there was Ronnie, feeling like shit, coming round and having to face it all again.

Suicide brought up so many feelings for Ash. It might be easier if it was unknown to him. He could understand why somebody would feel it was all too much and that the rewards were just not enough. That was another thing he wanted to talk to Renée about. Talking it through was the only thing that helped at the moment, especially how he had missed the signs.

He approached a roundabout and saw Geraldine's foot press on the imaginary brake. Why couldn't he say, 'For Christ's sake, drive if you want to but if not, get your bloody attitude out of the car!' She wasn't that brilliant a driver, but he'd never criticized her, instead just boiled inside.

Tom didn't look good. Physically he looked healthy enough. Skin good, if a little pale. Hair tidy, but he looked thin. The brief chat they'd had with him before seeing his psychiatrist had only convinced Ash of the emptiness Tom was feeling. He seemed pleased to see them but none of them were really able to say what they wanted, and Tom was jumpy. Ash noticed though, a softness in how Geraldine was with Tom.

The psychiatrist was young and pretty and, Ash sensed, genuine in her concern for Tom. He felt without her having to say, that Geraldine felt she was too young. She said that Tom was doing well and beginning to open up and to think about whether he could make the necessary changes in his life.

As she talked Ash felt some envy that this young woman could talk to Tom in a way that he couldn't and remembered the abortive last stay. Sitting on the unfamiliar side of the desk, he felt dazed and answerless, simply a confused parent, sad and a bit hopeless.

They followed Tom across the garden to his room. He was pleased to see that it was comfortable and modern. The grounds were well kept and spacious. Ash found himself thinking briefly of Ronnie and his own feelings of despair. Why did life have to be so hard? It wasn't a game. They were all reasonable people who just sometimes found the task too much.

When the balance of the mind was disturbed.

There was only so much pressure anybody could take. Geraldine talked and asked questions and he wondered if they would talk on the way home. He wanted to know what she thought about Tom but if he brought it up, it would undoubtedly end up with him feeling that so much was his fault, and the sadness and despair would begin. He seemed unable to stop the guilt these conversations induced. She had been a good mother, maybe their tensions had had more effect than they realised.

It was difficult to leave Tom. There were a couple of others about his age, but Tom was diffident about them. He was finding the group work difficult and he was clearly depressed. Ash was disappointed. It was as if Tom didn't care. He guessed though, that Tom knew that any change he made now was for life, and that was not easy. He was bound to be depressed. Up till now all the things he associated with fun, had involved alcohol or drugs.

The journey home seemed quicker and they didn't talk much. Claire was coming down in a couple of weeks and they made arrangements to go out for a meal. Geraldine had chosen a restaurant he didn't particularly like, but he didn't feel strongly enough to protest. It would be good to see Claire. He loved his sensible, single-minded daughter, and he looked forward to seeing his one child who didn't give him any worry.

The answerphone was flashing when he got back from dropping Geraldine. He pressed the key. It gave its jarring bleep, then he heard Arnold's voice.

'Ash …' the line was bad. 'Ash, Renée asked me to phone you. I'm afraid she's fallen and broken her hip. You had an appointment with her on Wednesday. Obviously she will have to cancel. She's OK, by the way. Well, as she can be. She's in The Royal Orthopaedic. Sorry about this. Not sure how long she'll be in. Oh … it's Arnold by the way.'

Ash put down the phone holding it onto the cradle. The immediate panic subsided, to be replaced by sadness, and then, fury. He needed her. How could she be so stupid as to do this now?

He grabbed hold of the table and steadied himself. It was OK. She wasn't dead. She had just broken her hip. He was sweating and shocked by his response. How bloody dependent was he? She had broken her hip. His concern should be for her. She would be uncomfortable and cross with herself, and irritated that she would be off work. It helped, putting himself in her shoes. But he felt bereft too. So much was happening. He didn't want to manage without her.

Chapter 41

If Jessica had been able to plan the progress of her protégé, she might have questioned the wisdom of putting Ash and Brenda in such close proximity. That Brenda was relating better and had more understanding of her own and other people's feelings was clear, but this obsession, this misdirected love, was complicated and something she hadn't anticipated.

By now she was familiar with the block of flats where Brenda lived. Moving north from the centre of the town, the houses got more and more worn-down looking, faded glory and nice proportions but the lack of curtains or a duvet cover masquerading as a curtain was a give away. Near Brenda's block, an old man sat, day after day, looking out, a white cat by his side. In the next window was a collection of teddy bears and a vase with a rose, the same flower week after week suggesting the bloom was plastic, and the half full lemonade bottle yellowing around the meniscus. Often Brenda waved to the man with the cat, but tonight his window was empty.

Brenda climbed the three steps to the front door. Inside she walked to the last of the five doors in the corridor. She carried her shopping inside the flat and put the bags on the kitchen table. She went into the sitting room, touching the storage heater as she passed. The flat smelt damp, Jessica noted. Back in the kitchen, Brenda unpacked a lasagne for one, some tomatoes, a loaf and some spread. She put milk in the fridge and reaching up, put three tins of cat food into the cupboard. In the cupboard under the sink, she put a bag of cat litter.

What, Jessica wondered, would Brenda do with her evening? Would it be the usual, television, supper, endless cups of tea and then television off and bed? It was hard for Jessica to feel inspired by Brenda's life. What did Brenda need to help her begin to find her potential?

But what was she doing now? Brenda had taken a spiral notebook from the drawer and sitting at the table, began to write:

Thursday 23rd. Didn't go to the group today. I didn't want to. He won't acknowledge our feeling. It's our secret.

In capitals she wrote her name. Underneath she wrote ASH JONES. She drew a large heart round the names. She wrote the names again, matching the letters and putting a line through the ones that were the same. B R E̲ N̲ D A̲ C H̲ I T. A̲ S̲ H̲ J O N̲E̲ S.

She crossed out the E's. Then the N's, the A's and the H's. Starting with her own name, she touched the letters that were left with her pen and saying to herself: he loves me, B; he loves me not, R; he loves me, D; he loves me not, C; he loves me, I. She did the same with Ash's name. He loves me, he loves me not, he loves me, he loves me not. In disgust she tore out the page, screwed it up and threw it on the floor.

In the kitchen she put the lasagne into the microwave.

Now, sitting on the settee, she opened a different notebook with a velvety cover. The Vecpoint pen was in the penholder. She began to write.

He loves me. I know that, Jessica read. He can't say and I don't really want him to, yet. The meeting with him was really difficult but what else could he do? I am annoyed though. He could have given a bit more indication. Glad I didn't go to the group on Thursday. It would have been too much. It was silly of him to say I could talk about it in the group. I suppose he has to say something. I don't really want to go to the group anymore but, if I don't I won't see him, so I suppose I will have to go. She left a line, then wrote,

> *You are my life and my love.*
> *You are the trees and the sky*
> *You are the blue flowers that edge the road*
> *I see your presence in spring yet*
> *You are the autumn colours too*
> *You are my life, my love, my all.*
> *I love you.*

She shut the notebook and slipped the pen back in its holder. Taking a different pen, she began *The Mail* crossword, and finished it in less that ten minutes. Under the pile of papers was a copy of *The Guardian* but that crossword was not tried, Jessica imagined Brenda believed it would be too hard for her.

Brenda unlocked the door leading to the back of the house. She stood for a moment, looking out over the patch of gravel where the dustbins were stored.

'Jonesie,' she called. 'Jone ... sie.' A thin tabby cat scrabbled over the fence and ran up to her, winding itself around her legs. Picking it up she held it close to her face, fondled its ears and scratched its neck. The cat purred contentedly, then wriggled to be put down. She followed the cat inside and locked the outer door.

Jessica caught her breath. Was this where the life was? With the cat, Brenda was normal, happy, and affectionate. Perhaps with animals she could be real. She remembered the sad house of Brenda's upbringing. Had there been a cat? Might that have been the one significant thing that had meant something to her as a little girl? It certainly needed fostering.

Chapter 42

It was one of those warm autumn days. Ash having opened the window now wondered whether the room was cold. At least the smell of paint was less strong. The group was silent. Through the door the phone trilled. He heard Rosemary's voice.

'The Firs – Good morning.' There was a pause. 'It's the decorators … They've been held up. Can't get here till this afternoon.'

Ash was sitting opposite the window. Outside birds sang. A butterfly flew in through the window. It settled for a moment on the ledge. A Red Admiral. It opened and closed its wings, then flew into the room. It flew up into the corner. Above Linda's head the butterfly flitted for a moment then paused and settled on her hair. Perfectly still, it perched. The sunlight filtered through the top strands of hair. The butterfly and the light on the hair. Ash stared at it, delighted.

The clock ticked. The butterfly left its resting place and flew up towards the ceiling. Ash guilty at his preoccupation, glanced round the group. The butterfly reappeared. It alighted on Peter's shoulder. It stayed perfectly still. Ash looked round. Hadn't anybody else seen it? Steph was staring at the window. Carl rested his chin in his hands.

The butterfly flew out of Ash's vision. What a beautiful creature. It returned and settled on Peter's chair. It boldly opened and shut its wings. Such colours. Peter moved his arm. Deftly the butterfly flew upwards. In a shaft of sunlight the dust danced. Nobody spoke. Ash brushed his cheek. He felt the softness of the tiny wings. He saw the butterfly rest once more on the window ledge. It opened and closed its wings and then it was gone.

Chapter 43

The invitation for supper had been in his diary for weeks. Ash had glanced at it several times, meaning to phone and cancel, but now he'd left it too late. Ralph and Trudi were old friends and he liked their company, but today he didn't have the interest or the energy.

He wanted to be able to talk about how shit he felt but that was not acceptable at a dinner party. Part of him rebelled at this, a sure indication that he was becoming ungrounded. Appropriateness was always one of the things that went when he was feeling low. All he wanted to do was read the paper, watch some television and sleep. Even music wasn't helping him at the moment. He couldn't listen to an entire piece, single notes would jar with him and whatever he chose was not the right piece or the right type of music. Nothing was right.

He opened the cupboard to choose a shirt. There'd been a ritual about clothes when he was with Geraldine. He'd found it demeaning. . The way she laid his clothes out for him. Like a child, but he'd supposed it was kind of her. He pulled a striped shirt out of the cupboard. He knew that he would find conversation difficult tonight. Usually a few drinks and he could chat like the rest of them, but in this mood, he felt flat and blank, his mind empty.

He drove around the by-pass finding driving strangely irksome. The lights seemed over-bright and even with his glasses he seemed to see objects at the side of the road that weren't there. Another sign of age, he supposed. He parked and sat in the car for a few minutes, wishing even at this late juncture, that he could phone and say he couldn't make it, but there was also the hope that, once there, once socialising, he would feel better. He picked up the bottle of wine and locked the car.

He hardly tasted the food. There were two other couples and a woman that he guessed he'd been paired with. 'Who shall we invite for Ash?' She was, predictably, fairly unattractive with a divorcee husband whose injustice to her she wanted to talk about, and an intense personality. His tolerance was tested as he listened to her story and avoided looking at her crêpey cleavage. God, he was unkind tonight. She really was a very nice woman but tonight, seeing Ralph and Trudi gave him a cloying feeling. Their happiness, their couplesie smugness. He managing to stay for the coffee, but he excused himself at eleven. Any longer and he would have screamed.

The night was crisp and starlit. He drove home and sank into bed, grateful that tomorrow was Sunday.

He woke in a frightened state. He felt unsettled, aware that he'd had a drink the night before and with a sense of dread that he associated with gathering depression. Had it been coming on for some time and, as often before, he hadn't noticed? He got up, made coffee and stirred through a bowl of sawdust-like muesli. Part of his Sunday ritual was to go and get the paper, spend an exorbitant amount of time reading it and stroll to the pub at lunchtime to chat to Toby and the usual crowd. That was beyond him today. He thought of returning to bed, but managed to stop himself.

The depression circling his heart was taking hold. What was there to feel good about? Look at his life. He was divorced. Tom was a drunk. His darling daughter was dead. His relationship with Eva was flimsy, and that was probably his fault. He'd fucked up with Ali so he couldn't even phone her, and there was the Brenda Chit business and now she was acting out, not attending the group. Then there was Ronnie. Even bloody Renée had deserted him. He felt really alone and had no energy.

He thought of next week, the enquiry, listening endlessly, the lack of fun and interest, and the boredom. It was no good. He couldn't face it. He was due some leave. He could phone Barry tomorrow; even if it was the week-end, say he needed some time. Nobody was indispensable. What about Leila? He'd phone her. She could decide whether she wanted to run the group on her own. If not, Rosemary could cancel them. It was not good practice but, like this, he was no good to anyone.

He was too tired to pack tonight. He would get up in time tomorrow. Make the phone calls and go to the cottage. He needed some time. That way he could perhaps contain this bout, get over it and nobody need know.

Chapter 44
The cottage

Ash was doing less and less. He'd come to the cottage to take stock of things and to get on top of the reports. On the first morning, he'd got up slowly, didn't bother to shave and pulling up a chair, picked up his pen. *Brenda Chit. Two Monthly Report'.*

He shook the pen. It wasn't right. He fetched the bottle of brown ink and went through the ceremony of filling it. He'd been pleased to find the ink, left from a previous visit, at the back of the cupboard. He wiped the nib clean and pulled the report towards him. *Thank you for the referral of your patient ...*

His writing didn't seem to respond to his instructions. It was untidy, unclear. He wished he could use his laptop but the electricity was still off.

He didn't know what to say. That was why he couldn't do it. He didn't know what to say about Brenda. A now familiar feeling of ennui was creeping up, sitting on his shoulder, waiting to be invited in. He shivered, got up and walked across the room. He reached for his jacket hanging behind the door and took out a half bottle. He unscrewed the top and took a deep swig. He noted that it was only nine thirty. Why had he felt so lonely and alone that he had to take himself off to this remote spot in the hope of finding some peace?

He'd thought about phoning someone, asking if he could stay. They might have been pleased, but he visualised the phone call, the chat, the request, the drive, the hello's, sitting down with a drink and then realising that he was bored.

He liked the idea of being with friends, needed them, but, increasingly, after about half an hour his mind would start to wander, a terrible restlessness would overcome him and he would want to go. Going out for a meal would start off well, then somewhere between the main course and pudding, he would be fighting the wish to leave, screamingly irritated by what others were saying, noticing every repeated story and silly remark. He wanted to be on his own, but now his own company was hardly bearable.

For a week he remained in this small contained space. One barely-managed trip to the local shop provided bread, eggs, and a bottle of whiskey. He often didn't dress, sometimes walking naked round the cottage. He felt answerable to no one. He became preoccupied with his bodily functions. He noticed if he was hungry. At work eating was so often dictated by the clock. If he was tired, he allowed himself to sleep. He peed long and luxuriously – enjoying the steady, strong flow. Recently he had worried that the miserable dribble he managed during his working day was an indication of his advancing years. He snored, waking himself up and he farted uncaringly. The remoteness of the cottage was what he had craved. Its nearness to the cliffs, an edge.

On some days the electricity came on for an hour. He'd found candles and matches but he couldn't organise food. There were a few apples on the tree and he'd found an old box of cereal. The fruit pie and sandwich he had arrived with, he took pleasure in making last, eating a small section each day as if on rations. The effort of getting in the car, going to the shop, deciding what to eat, seemed less and less possible. Perhaps he would just not eat. He wasn't very hungry but he only had a bit of whiskey left. The opened bottle of wine he'd found in the cupboard over the sink had long gone.

The storm broke at about six. A huge clap of thunder took out the lights. Heavy rain thundered on the roof and a window banged upstairs. He ought to see to it. Lightning lit up the room. Out of the window shadows leapt into focus and disappeared.

He'd so often come to the cottage because of its closeness to the sea – but there'd always been somebody else before. He was cold. He hadn't lit a fire. He knew there was wood outside but by now it would be soaked. He felt terribly alone ... like a lonely child ... A clap of thunder made him jump. He was shaking, giving into fear. He took the flask, sat in the corner of the sofa, and pulled the rug around him. It smelt. He was crying. He saw himself, an old man, shivering, alone, wrapped in a smelly rug unable to help himself.

The light woke him. The air felt clear after the storm. His mouth felt awful. For the first time in days, he lit the boiler and ran water for a bath. He found wood and put it ready for a fire. He fried an egg and made some toast. He felt better but completely withdrawn. He wasn't sure which day it was. He turned on his mobile and put it on the table.

The mobile shuddered and rang. Its ring pierced the room. Angrily he punched it off. Who would call him? He didn't want to speak to anyone. The phone lay there. He opened the front door and looked across the field to the cliffs. His eyes saw the beauty but it didn't touch him. He glanced back at the phone. Then he walked over and picked it up. He dialled one two one. A voice said,

'Where the fuck are you? Why didn't you say you were taking leave? Are you OK? Call me!' It was Ali.

It had stopped raining. Ash took his coat from the car and set off along the path. His sleep had been troubled by disturbing dreams. Underfoot the grass was slippery from the rain. He looked out over the sea. The air was not quite clear of mist. He took the path that snaked down towards a small cove. His feet slipped on the shale and several times he slithered, catching onto roots and vegetation edging the path.

He still had no wish for company. At times in the past he'd been troubled by his need for others and yet his wish to shun them. He knew that people saw him as independent. Today he felt he had turned a corner. The awful need to have somebody around had passed and he was happy to be on his own. Now he could finish the reports and enjoy his last few days here.

His foot slipped Shale cascaded around him. He grabbed a root. It broke. He lost his footing. Sliding, careering he saw a large rock. He was sliding straight towards it. His knee crashed into it. Pain shot up his leg.

He came to, aware of cold sweat. His knee throbbed badly and if he moved the pain shot up his leg. He looked around him. The sea was distant and tranquil below, the cliff path above. There was nobody in sight. The first moment of panic ran through him. Apart from the farmer who owned the cottage, he had never seen anybody on his walks. His new found independence began to evaporate, and he was the frightened child again.

He opened his eyes and saw the dog. It was outlined on the top of the cliff. Dog – man, his logic said. He called stupidly,

'Dog – here boy.'

The effort of shouting hurt his ribs. The dog disappeared and he lay back closing his eyes.

A shower of stones shook him. The dog came up to him. Relief seared through him.

'Here boy – good boy.'

The dog allowed himself to be fussed. His tail wagging. Ash looked round. Perhaps the dog had an owner. The dog snuffled about sending small stones downwards. Ash didn't want the dog to go, its steady brown eyes comforted him. The dog turned and scampered back up the path. With the dog seemed to go all hope.

Clouds were gathering overhead. He was cold and his watch told him an hour had passed. It began to dawn on him that he might not be rescued. In that instant, survival kicked in. He didn't want to be a news item. He rolled over, closing his eyes with the pain and pulled himself onto all fours. He couldn't put any weight on his right knee but half crawling, half dragging, he began to pull himself back up the path.

After ten minutes he had moved less than twenty metres from the rock. He was now very cold. He looked to the top of the cliff and as if a metaphor for his life, the top seemed unreachable, the task too difficult. He wrapped his arms around himself and lay still.

A stone hit his face. He looked up. A man's frame was silhouetted against the sky. The dog next to him. They disappeared and Ash gave a thin cry. They reappeared and another shower of stones clattered past as the man started to scramble down the path towards him.

Chapter 45

Leila put a chair out for Ash even though he wasn't going to be there. Getting the room ready helped with her nervousness. She didn't put flowers on the table, that seemed such an 'Ash' thing to do, and it didn't feel right to do it. Besides she hadn't brought any.

At ten o'clock she went down to the group room and was dismayed to see that nobody was there. She'd heard noises from the kitchen and hoped it was the group members. She sat for a while wondering what she would do if nobody turned up. It was odd. It had never happened before. They couldn't have known Ash wouldn't be here, could they?

Carl and Peter appeared at the door. They took seats next to each other then sat quietly, looking at the floor. Leila's heart was pounding. All the excitement had gone and she just felt a bit sick. Steph came in next, followed by Linda and Ronnie. Ronnie looked pale but had on his usual neat grey trousers and jumper that looked as if it had been ironed. They took seats and sat quietly. April came in next and then Norma arrived, a bit flustered. Leila thought it best to wait until they were all there to tell them about Ash.

'Sorry, the bus was late. Sorry.' She took a seat. 'Sorry.' She nodded and smiled at everyone.

After five minutes nobody had spoken. Five minutes was nothing but for Leila today, it felt endless.

'Dr Jones is late,' said Carl. Leila was about to explain, when there was a knock on the door and Brenda came in. Leila waited until Brenda sat down.

'I'm afraid that Dr Jones won't be here today,' she said. 'He had to go somewhere important. He sends his apologies.' That sounded all wrong, like they weren't important.

'Shall we go then?' said Steph.

'Why?' said Leila, then regretted it. It sounded defensive.

'Well, if he isn't here, there's no point is there?' said Steph.

'You're all here,' said Leila, but wasn't brave enough to add, 'and so am I.' Ash, she was sure, would have said nothing and waited to see what happened.

'It's not right,' said Linda. 'Ronnie's only just come back after, you know. Dr Jones should be here. Aren't we important?'

'Will he be here next week?' Brenda asked. She looked upset.

'As far as I know,' said Leila. 'But we're here and I'm wondering what other feelings are around.'

'… other feelings are around,' she heard Steph mimic. She tried to ignore it but she felt terrible. If she spoke it sounded wrong. If she said nothing, what would happen? And she was hurt. Didn't her presence mean anything? She glanced at Norma, realising that she was hoping for some support but Norma was looking down and seemed a bit fidgety.

'There's no flowers,' said Carl. He looked thoughtful. 'Does he do the flowers then?' He was looking at her. Leila tried to think. It was important to think what was behind the question, but the trouble was, she couldn't think. They were looking at her.

'What do you think?' she said at last. Carl shrugged. Nobody seemed interested in pursuing it. Not such a good answer after all.

'I know he does the flowers,' said Brenda quietly.

'How do you know?' said Steph. Brenda didn't say anything.

'Have you seen him?' Peter asked. Brenda looked down.

'Have you?' persisted Steph. Still Brenda said nothing. 'Because if you haven't it's a silly thing to say.' Brenda shot Steph a look of pure venom.

Leila felt worried. They weren't often this scratchy. Why did it have to happen this week? Norma said,

'I've got something I want to say. Is that all right?' Leila thanked her silently. 'I want to know how you – meet people.' Norma looked round the room.

'What do you mean?' said Ronnie. Leila was pleased that he'd spoken. Last week, he'd hardly said a word.

'When I was in the convent, I was lonely sometimes but there were always people around. Now I hardly talk to anybody unless I'm at work and there's really only me and my boss and at weekends I don't really see anybody. I go to church, of course, but after that, well, I'm on my own. I chat to people, but they always seem to be in a hurry to get away.' Norma half smiled then looked sad. 'I'm interested in them, but they never ask about me.'

'I know what you mean,' said April. Norma looked at April as if surprised that she understood.

'I don't think I could go to the cinema on my own and I want to help at the shelter again, but it all feels so different – now. I feel I've lost my protection and I get quite flustered if men talk to me. When I was in my habit, I could talk to anyone. I'm usually all right with women but there's this man ...' She stopped.

'You're all right with us,' Peter said.

'Oh, you're different,' said Norma. Peter made a face at Ronnie.

'This man ...? said Carl.

'Yes, I see him at church. He's always been very friendly. He's quite nice. I think.'

'Surely you know if he's nice or not,' said Steph.

'But I don't Steph. What I mean is other people seem to think he's quite nice, but they don't want to talk to him. I notice that. He is a bit – dull.'

'You're not sure if you want to be more friendly, or if it's just that you are lonely,' Leila ventured.

'Yes,' said Norma empathically. 'That's it exactly.' Norma looked round at them as if expecting advice.

'Sometimes I wonder if anyone here would talk to me if we weren't in the group,' Peter said.

'Oh, I would,' said Norma. 'I feel I know you ... I trust you all.'

'Steady on Norma,' said Steph. 'You'll be saying you like us next.'

'But I do,' Norma started, and then seeing that Steph was teasing, she stopped. 'Yes, maybe I'm too naïve.'

'Too naïve to trust people in the group?' said Leila. Norma gave a half smile.

'I don't trust anybody,' said April. 'It's stupid to.'

'Don't you trust anybody here?' Carl asked.

'I trust Dr Jones – and Leila,' she said. Leila felt that last was a concession. 'I don't like it without Dr. Jones,' April said. 'It doesn't feel right.'

'Perhaps you don't feel you can trust me, like you can him,' Leila said.

'Well, he's in charge, isn't he? You're only a ...' she stopped.

'A what?' said Leila, suddenly a bit angry and feeling bolder.

'Well, what are you?' Steph asked. 'Are you going to be a therapist?'

'I hope so,' said Leila, 'one day. I know you miss Dr Jones but it's as if you don't think you could help each other without him being here.'

'Well,' said Peter, 'He's like the father, isn't he?' Once again Leila said a silent thanks for this insight.

'Like a father?' said Leila.

'Not like mine,' said Brenda.

'Or mine,' said April.

'Well, he's not my father and I think it is wrong that he is not here. It's been a complete waste of time this week,' said Linda. Leila resisted reacting.

'No it hasn't,' said Norma. 'I feel much better for having told you about my … problem.'

'You should try internet dating Norma,' said Steph. 'But I want to know how you know about Dr Jones and the flowers,' said Steph turning to Brenda. Brenda didn't answer. Her neck was red. 'How do you know?' Steph was staring at Brenda.

'I just do,' she said. 'but I don't want to talk about it.' Brenda was now very red. Leila was resisting rescuing her though she looked so uncomfortable. Suddenly Brenda stood up.

'It's stupid here without Dr Jones. You're right Linda, it's a waste of time and I don't see the point of staying.' She took her coat off the back of the chair and picking up her bag, left the room.

'What was all that about?' said Steph. Leila wasn't sure if she should go after Brenda, or send someone else. Then Linda stood up.

'I'm going too. This is silly.' To Leila's dismay, she too picked up her coat and left the room.

'I'll stay,' said Carl, and Ronnie nodded. Leila was horrified to feel tears building. She mustn't cry.

'It seems that without Dr Jones it all seems a bit pointless but I think you may be upset because Dr Jones is away and you have been left with the baby sitter, and it reminds you of other times when you were being abandoned by somebody important.'

'No, it's because it's his group,' said Steph disparagingly.

'I think I know what Leila is getting at,' said Ronnie gently. 'Is it because several of us have had fathers who weren't there or not much, is that why you think Dr Jones is so important to us?' Leila looked at him with gratitude and amazement.

'Does that make sense to you, Ronnie?' she said. He nodded. Suddenly she felt vindicated. This was what it was all about.

'Can we go early?' said April. 'Look it's nearly time.' In panic Leila looked at the clock. There was still twenty minutes to go. 'It's not time yet,' she said. April shrugged and reached for her coat. 'Sorry,' she said. Steph was doing the same. Leila was losing control of the tears. She looked imploringly at the men.

'We might as well go too,' said Ronnie, 'Sorry.'

'Shall I stay?' said Carl, as the others walked to the door. Leila shook her head. Better to let him go. 'Shall I shut the door?' Leila nodded.

Then the tears fell. She couldn't stop them. What a disaster. What would Ash say? How had she ever thought she could run a group, and now she had to get out to her car without people seeing that she had been crying. What if she'd spoiled Ash's group. Suppose they didn't come back? Sod Ash. Why did he have to leave her alone with this?

Chapter 46

It was Sunday, a week since he had returned from the cottage. His knee was well strapped but he still found walking difficult. You were lucky – the doctor had told him but the new trauma, added to the old rugby injury, might mean a cartilage operation in the future. His ribs were still uncomfortable and he still felt a bit battered, but, with the pain and the inconvenience, came depression.

Everywhere he looked Ash saw people getting on with their lives. The more he saw the more stuck he felt. For the umpteenth time Ash rooted around thinking of people he knew that he might be able to talk to. Someone who would listen and understand, but it always came back to the same thing. How could he tell them how he really felt, without them despising him? All respect gone. Although he was in dull torment, for the moment nobody knew, and it felt important to preserve that, though when Ronnie had talked about how he'd felt, Ash had found it quite difficult not to say, in a way that might convey more than professional empathy, that he knew what he meant. At times he felt he didn't care if people knew, but then, if the pain subsided a little, he was grateful that his despair was still hidden.

None of it made sense. Up till now there'd always been a point. A reason to continue. Helping people to make themselves better. But feeling like this, he couldn't even help himself. Did it work anyway? Why not slap everybody on medication? Some at least would be happier. It would be good to get out of the city.

A small detour and he would be by the dockyard. He could find a pub and have lunch near the water. The fantasised pub was not to be found though and he contented himself with a sandwich from a filling station and coffee in a paper cup. He parked with a small boat-yard in view. There was not much activity except a man in blue overalls, painting the hull of a wooden boat. Skilfully the man painted dark blue up to the bow line. Ash wondered if the man was married or widowed.

It began to drizzle. The man became blurred. Ash turned on the engine and put on the wipers. It seemed important to see the man leave. The man climbed down the ladder carrying the paint and walked into a wooden building. Ash turned off the engine.

What would it be like to have a job like that? To have a task, complete it, and go home. He used to spend a lot of time tinkering with his car. At the end of a morning, he would have a real sense of achievement. Now he had no time and no workshop and these days, his car was maintained by the garage. He could spend an enjoyable fifteen minutes talking to the mechanic but he appreciated that engines were much more complicated now and he wasn't sure whether he could do even the simple jobs he used to do. The smell of the garage and the echoey sounds of the workshop still evoked happy times. The brain was a sort of engine, he reflected, but not so easy to mend or diagnose.

He'd always longed to belong. Most people did, but feeling like this mitigated against it. Feel good and others want to be with you. Feel low and nobody wanted to know. He just wanted someone to talk to, but who? Renée was still recovering and it was still awkward with Ali.

How did other people manage to be happy? It had not been until a few years ago that he'd even considered being happy a viable ambition. He wouldn't want many of their lives but he would like their contentment.

This sodding illness. He hated the way it got him by the throat filling his head with these obsessive, maudlin thoughts. Most worrying was that it made him tearful. He put his head in his hands. A grown man crying and not only that – somebody who was supposed to make others better. What a fraud he was. He took a handkerchief from his pocket and gave a loud blow.

He put the car into neutral and turned on the engine. This was not working. He'd go back and resort to the usual panacea – sleep.

Ash woke from his sleep. The paper was scattered over the table and the rug had slipped off his legs. He felt cold and his neck ached where he had slept awkwardly. He was still caught in his dream. In it he was in a part of his life he had almost forgotten, with people he had not thought about for years. It was as if he no longer knew himself. A dread like annihilation gripped his stomach.

He got up and put the central heating on for an hour. Usually he used his dreams as pointers but this one made no sense. He went to the desk, unlocking the third drawer, took out a box of tablets and went to the kitchen for some water. He put the glass and the tablets on the table. He rued the day he had taken his first tablet though at the time, they had served a purpose. Did he want to start on them again?

He went into the kitchen and washed his face. On the patio a shaft of sunlight lit up the red brilliance of a geranium. The plants on the patio looked good. He drank the last of the water, picked up the tablets, went back into the sitting room, put the tablets back in the drawer and locked it.

For the first time in days something lifted. Perhaps he could try and believe in what he knew, without resorting to the medication. He turned on the radio. Art Tatum was playing 'Have you met Miss Jones?' Ash found himself singing.

He washed up a couple of cups and the business last week with lost files came into his mind. Everybody had been so jumpy, nobody wanting to accept any blame. He'd prayed that it wouldn't turn out that he had filed them in the wrong place. Then in the afternoon Rosemary had pushed open the door and said,

'Dr Jones. We've found them. They were at the back of the cupboard. We had them all the time. We just didn't realise.' Suddenly he understood why this had come into his mind. It was Rosemary's words.

'We had them all the time … we just didn't realise'. Is that how it was? It wasn't out there belonging to other people. It was here – in him. He had it here all the time.

He'd warmed up. It really was very cosy in his flat. He picked up the paper and turned to this evening's television. There was even a half decent film that he might lose himself in.

Chapter 47

They sat next to each on the slightly battered leather sofas. Although it was quite crowded downstairs, up here, they and the couple in the corner were the only people. This was another wine bar Ali had found. It was a change from the usual stainless steal and glass and had wooden panelling and stone-edged windows. The lighting was softer, large lazy plants looked permanent and in the background, Peggy Lee sang 'Aren't you kinda glad we did?' It made Ash smile. He didn't think Ali noticed. He was delighted that this had happened without any engineering on his part. They had simply met at the door and he'd readily agreed to Ali's friendly suggestion that they go for a drink. They hadn't talked much since the evening at her flat but things seemed to have softened and tonight it felt like old times.

They sat quite close, but the frisson of their last meeting seemed to have gone, not, Ash felt, that it couldn't be fanned into life quite easily. He noticed too, that she wasn't drinking as if her life depended on it and after half an hour she hadn't gone out for a cigarette. The explanation came soon enough.

'I'm giving up,' she said. 'Not today, but that's the plan. You know how it is, first you need to be alert to something, then change can happen.' She laughed, throwing back her head.

'That's good,' said Ash. 'What's brought that about?'

'It's no fun any more. No fun huddled outside in the rain and the cold. Not that I think it is fair, but it will save me money – but I'm going for one now. I'll get another bottle.' The drinking wasn't slowing down that much then. It would be a taxi job again.

It was so good to be at the end of the week and temporarily leave work behind. He wondered if Ali might be somebody who understood. She might even know. She always noticed if he was withdrawn, and they'd been friends a long time, but there were still things they didn't talk about. Maybe they both felt some shame. What they got from each other was an escape from the responsibility and worries. It suited them both. If he burdened her with his depression, she might feel she had to do something about it. Consider what she said. They spent their whole lives doing that. As it was, she could say what she liked and it freed him up too. No, it was good as it was. It was a strange business though. In some ways he could say anything to her but something as important as this, he chose to keep unsaid.

Ali returned and flopped down on the settee. She touched his arm as she leaned forward for her drink, but this was a different touch. It was friendly and warm. Who knew what might happen in the future, but for now it seemed as if their old comradeship had returned and it felt safe and close.

Chapter 48

It was the second week that Brenda had not been at the group, and there was no message. Ash didn't usually respond to one week's absence; there could be so many reasons, but after two missed sessions, he knew he ought to make contact. She had not said anything about her feelings in the group and was increasingly sullen and unresponsive. By Friday there was still no message, so he decided to send a letter.

Dear Brenda, Sorry you have not been able to get to the group for the last two weeks. I hope things are well with you and I look forward to seeing you next Thursday.

The letter would go with the afternoon post. She would probably get it on Saturday.

She did not appear at the next meeting. Norma asked if he had heard from her, but there was no further interest in her absence, which Ash took as an indication of their hostility to her recent withdrawal.

Reluctantly, he now felt he must speak to her. He was aware too, of Leila's scrutiny. When he did phone, Brenda's tone was flat.

'Hello.'

'Brenda, this is Dr Jones. I am phoning to see why you have not been at the group.' There was a pause. 'Brenda, I don't want to pressure you but…'

'You know why.'

'What do you mean?'

'I can't come to the group because I don't want to talk about it to them. I only want to talk to you. I told you all that.' Ash waited, then said,

'You haven't felt able to bring it to the group?' There was an intake of breath.

'I've told you. If I can't talk to you on your own, I am not coming back to the group.' Ash felt cornered but almost before he could think, he said.

'All right. I could see you at nine fifteen on Friday.' Did he detect a slight glee in her voice matched only by his sickening feeling?

Brenda put on her blue dress. She tied her hair back into a tight, thin, tail. Although a small part of her knew her thoughts were fantasy, a bigger part was taking over, visualising the scene when, finally realising that he was unable to resist, Ash would pull the ribbon from her hair to let it tumble over her shoulders. She smiled to herself at this. Her hair wasn't long enough to tumble, for God's sake.

Unquestioningly she loved him. He occupied her waking and often her sleeping thoughts and in her dreams, she could see their future. She knew it might be difficult but she'd heard of it happening. Teachers and pupils, therapists and patients. Of course she would have to stop being his patient, but if they were together she would have no need to be his patient. She would be happy. Perhaps they could start with meeting for a drink. She put her hand over the delicious quivering in her stomach. She sat, eyes unfocussed, lost in thought. It wasn't that he was particularly good looking, but that was the thing with love, beauty was in the eye of the beholder. If that was true, she shouldn't care about how she looked, but she worried that he would see her as too skinny or dull looking. She stood up. She could wear the blue earrings. They would match the dress and she'd often noticed how matching colours could make an impact.

Chapter 49
Omission

Ash felt that every time he looked up, he caught Leila's eye. It was his guilt of course. It couldn't have been clearer if she'd said, what's going on with Brenda? He'd missed their last week's supervision session because he was late, but it could have been avoided. He could have bought the paper later and the dry cleaning could have waited. He liked working with her, she had a welcome maturity but now he was being evasive and she as yet it seemed, hadn't summoned up the courage to say anything to him.

The trouble was he wouldn't know what to say. He could tell her that he had decided that in Brenda's best interest, he had decided to see her for a few individual sessions? Sounded OK, but then what about Norma or Ronnie who had asked for individual sessions but now no longer asked, understanding that that was not on offer. Why, she would wonder, had he made an exception for Brenda?

He could say, she has a fixation on me and I thought it best to work with it outside the group. True, but these things could so easily be misunderstood. He would rather manage it outside the group, get Brenda back in and nobody need be any the wiser. It hit him in a moment. What he was doing was just what Brenda was doing. He was not bringing it to the group. At another time he would have recognised it sooner. He would give a bit of thought to what he could say to Leila at the next supervision.

Ash opened the window and pulled two of the chairs opposite each other, putting one at a slight angle. A minute before time, there was a gentle knock on the door and Brenda came in. She smiled and sat down in the seat he indicated.

Brenda had on a blue dress and sparkling in her ears were bright blue earrings. They glinted as she moved. They were pretty and he thought how good they would look on Eva.

'I had another dream about you last night,' Brenda began. 'We were in some other country. It was warm and the sea was near. We walked along the beach and then you stopped and said, why don't we swim? Neither of us had costumes so we stripped off and ran into the water. When we were in the water, you pulled me towards you ...'

A chair scraped next door and Ash, unable to bear the rest of the dream, said,

'What do you make of this bit of your dream, Brenda?'

'There's more,' she said, the edge of irritation in her voice.

'Yes, I imagine there is, but perhaps we can look first at what this part of the dream might mean.' She looked at him boldly.

'It's obvious isn't it?' she said. 'Don't you call it a wish fulfilment dream?' She half smiled. Ash looked down, not wishing to enter into the flirtation.

'Yes, that's the context of the dream, but what do you think it might mean for you?' Brenda looked half quizzical and half perplexed. 'Do you have any thoughts about what the sea might mean in your dream?'

'Well, it's warm and soft and you can get lost in it.'

'Lost ...?'

'Yes ... No ... not lost, but ... you know. It holds you up ... supports you and it's all around you and you feel safe.'

'You can also drown in the sea.'

'Yes, but when it's warm and calm, it's OK. I love the sea.'

'You love the sea.'

'Yes, I'd like to be there with you. We could be close, touching. I could ...'

'Brenda,' he said, 'All of this, particularly your dream, has meaning for you but dreams aren't necessarily literal.'

'There you go again. Trying to make it what it is not. It seems perfectly clear to me. I just love you.' Tears were brimming in Brenda's eyes.'

'Have you ever felt like this before?' said Ash gently.

'In love you mean? No.'

'Can you ever remember having loving feelings towards anybody in your life?' Brenda thought for a moment.

'I loved my Gran,' she said. Ash nodded. 'But that's not the same. Not like this.'

'Is she still alive?' Ash asked.

'My Gran – no. She died when I was nine.'

'Tell me about her.'

'She used to make these scone things, with real jam and we could eat as many as we liked. Sandra, that's my sister, used to tell me not to take another but Gran would say, if you're hungry, have another. You'll know when you've had enough … and I did. You'd just get to where you couldn't eat any more.'

'She let you have as much as you wanted?' Ash said.

'Yes.' Brenda stared towards the window. 'She wore this holey grey cardigan. Not holey because it was old, but a sort of knitted pattern. She knitted all the time and it was … nice. We could read or play cards and there was this click, click, click in the background and they had a real fire and the coal had a smell … it was really cosy.'

'You liked it there.'

'Yes, said Brenda. 'I used to wish I could live with her. I said that once to my dad and he hit me. I didn't ask again. My Granddad was nice too. He smoked a pipe but he died when I was five. Gran was sort of sad for a while but she never stopped us going round there. Now I think about it, I think she liked having us there. That was what was so nice. You knew she wanted you there.'

'Sounds like she really loved you and your sister.'

'Yes. I was sad when she died. All the best things get taken away, don't they? I think life's a pig, most of the time.' She seemed to have come out of her reverie. 'Funny to be talking about my Gran, but that's not the sort of love I have for you.'

'It's not?'

'No … of course not.'

'It's all love.'

'Yes … but …'

'What does love mean to you, Brenda?'

'Well, it's when you think somebody is great and you want to be with them and they want to be with you.'

'Sounds a bit like you and your Gran.'

'Yes, but that's not the same.'

'Why not?'

'Well, I didn't want to sleep with my Gran.'

'No, but you felt cared for and wanted and … loved.'

'Yes, I suppose so.'

'Feeling loved by somebody when you are little, is very precious. You know that it's possible to be loved. It helps.'

The session was at an end.

'Why did you ask about my Gran?' said Brenda putting on her coat.

The door closed quietly behind her.

Chapter 50

Jessica, making her way to Brenda's flat, felt a tingling sensation. She moved untouched sidling through the crowd and stood for a moment, identifying the image that the tingling brought up. The image was Brenda, but a little Brenda, standing by a door and tentatively pushing it open.

Chapter 51

He arranged the next meeting with Brenda for an hour before the group, hoping that she might be persuaded to stay on. When he came downstairs, she was waiting in the hallway and didn't follow him into the room, but waited until he called her in.

Brenda sat, not saying anything. At last she said,

'I was thinking about what you said, last week, about love and what it was. I still think what I feel for you is different, but I suppose there are different sorts of love.' Ash waited. 'Then I was thinking abut sex ... well, sex and love. I'm not sure how they fit together. I mean, what I feel for you is love, I know that, but that wouldn't be enough. I want to make love to you. Have you make love to me. Have sex with you. That's what I call love.'

Ash thought for a moment. What was this young woman's experience of sex, he wondered? She sat, legs wound round each other, staring at him. If he asked her about her experience at this stage, would she interpret it as interest?

'You say you were thinking about love and what it means for you.'

'Not just me – us.'

'Brenda, there is no us. What you are feeling is understandable but our work here is to understand where these feeling come from. It isn't reality.'

'So you say,' she said sulkily.

He noticed an increasing ease with her. The beginning of being able to think in her presence. She was, he was realising, a surprisingly intelligent young woman. She was quick and perceptive, though not about her feelings about him. These remained fixed. It was a feeling he recognised. The moment when he could see somebody's potential, often before it was apparent to them.

One of the windows had been opened and he could hear the scrape, scrape, scrape of a rake on the gravel.

'I don't think you're listening to me,' Brenda said. Ash raised his eyebrows.

'What happens for you, Brenda ... when you think I am not listening to you?'

'I feel overlooked, like I'm taking up your time – boring you.'

'Anything else?'

'Yes. Angry. Were you listening or doing your shopping list?'

'Is this a familiar feeling?' Ash sidestepped. Brenda stared at him. A mixture of animosity and thoughtfulness.

'You want me to say that I have problems with anger, don't you?'

'I don't want you to say anything that doesn't make sense to you. Do you think you have problems with anger?'

'Don't you ever get angry?' Brenda said suddenly. 'I mean don't you get angry with the patients and that?' Ash thought of his ranting fury at the cottage.

'You wonder if I get angry? Would it help you if you thought I did?'

'Well, it might make you more real – not so saint-like.'

'Saint like. Is that how you see me?'

'Well, you are aren't you – a bit?'

'You sound angry Brenda. I wonder if you are angry with me?'

'Oh here we go. See if you could make me angry. Well, you won't. I'm not saying I don't get angry, but I wouldn't with you.'

There were footsteps outside the door and he remembered that he hadn't turned the occupied notice round. The door opened. Alison stood in the doorway.

Oh ... Dr Jones! Sorry, I thought ...' She stood for a moment, then the door banged shut. Unconsciously, Ash had jumped up.

Ali looked hurt. 'I couldn't believe it. I thought we'd been through all this ...'

'All what? What had we been through?'

'The Chit woman. It's bad enough she's still here and in your group. What the hell are you doing seeing her by herself?'

Ash was suddenly angry. What had it to do with her? He looked into her steely eyes and at that moment he hated her.

'Ali. I'm not going to talk about this now. It is my decision. I don't have to discuss everything with you. I have my reasons. Now let's leave it, please.' He left the room not sure where he was going. At a loss and not wanting to bump into anybody, he went out of the front door, got into his car his car, sinking thankfully into the driver's seat and closing his eyes.

She was right of course. Her words 'What the hell are you doing seeing her on her own?' seared into him. He was furious too that she had interrupted just when he was just getting somewhere with Brenda. Her barging in had left a jagged and awkward end to the session. He had just managed to arrange the next meeting before Brenda left the room.

The incident with Ali affected him more than he realised. He felt the familiar deadness in the pit of his stomach. How quickly it took hold. He was taking a risk but what else could he do? He couldn't abandon Brenda now. As for Ali, he was fed up with her moods and the proprietorial way she behaved towards him. Fuck her. He would do this his way.

He did little over the weekend and almost looked forward to Monday. The phone call, as he was about to leave for work, hit him like a blow

'It's Tom,' Geraldine said, 'he's collapsed. One of his so-called friends got him to A and E but he's in a bad way. The hospital has just rung. He's in Woolwich wherever that is. The nurse says he's OK there for the moment but would like one of us to go up as soon as possible. I think it is serious.'

After the initial clutch at his heart he was shocked at the irritation he felt at having to change his plans and surprised at Geraldine wanting them both to go. It was Brenda's appointment today, the first after Ali had barged in, but he would have to postpone it. Damn. And how serious was it? He had understood that Tom was doing OK. There hadn't been much contact but he had taken that as good.

Tom was yellow. He sat on one side of the bed, Geraldine on the other. They made desultory conversation. Claire had said she would come to the hospital and Ash was waiting for her arrival, hoping her presence might lighten the gloom. Tom had difficulty keeping his eyes open. Geraldine reaching for the flower vase, muttering that she was going to change the water. Ash looked at his son, gaunt, sunken cheeked.

Tom opened his eyes and looked at him. 'I thought I was winning, Dad,' he said. 'I felt so good. We were going to this houseboat thing. I'd met this really nice girl. It was all going so good ...' Geraldine returned with the flowers. She banged the vase down, plumping the flowers up once more. Tom had closed his eyes again.

Ash looked round. There was something so impersonal about a hospital ward. Your identity was only as a patient. Any further identity made by the illness you had. That's the diabetic, overdose, cancer in the corner. Ash thought about what Tom had said. He could remember the feeling, occasionally, when things were going well, slotting into place, when he was confident, unselfconscious, and Tom was young. How much more appropriate for him to feel it, except Tom's feeling was fuelled by alcohol and more, Ash suspected. Tom opened his eyes.

'Dad.' They craned forward. 'I ...' There was the squeak of heels approaching. Geraldine jumped up and kissed her daughter. Claire hugged him then went to Tom and kissed him gently on the forehead.

'What have you done to yourself now?' she said. They looked at each other. A single tear escaped down Tom's cheek.

It had been touch and go. Ash hardly dared engage with that. The sister had been factual but unsympathetic. Perhaps she had too much to do. It wasn't clear when Tom would be discharged. Ash did a mental diary check. If he had to come up and collect him, when could he do it and, the same vexed question, where would he go this time?

At the end of visiting time, they left the ward together. Geraldine would stay with her sister nearby and would visit again tomorrow when hopefully he would be discharged.

'Dad, can I have a lift?' Claire said. 'I came in by train today. It won't make you too late. Will it?' At the hospital entrance they said goodbye, just an ordinary family pecking goodbye on the cheek. As they walked towards the car park Claire slipped her arm through his. 'Shall we have tea dad, when we get back? I haven't seen you for ages and there won't be time to talk at the wedding. If we stop at Fulmers, I'll buy us a cake.' It felt childish and fun. Tea and cake.

The door of Claire's small terraced house had been painted blue since the last time he'd been there. The earth in the tiny garden recently dug and tubs neat with dark earth ready for spring bulbs There was a smell of sawn wood when she opened the door. They squeezed round each other in the neat narrow hallway.

He was pleased to see her white piano in the corner. He lifted the lid and tinkled a scale. He settled on the sofa while she made the tea. She appeared shortly with the cake on a tray, two small plates and a spotted teapot. There was an embroidered cloth on the tray. She set it down and sat on the sofa next to him.

'Do you get to play much?' he asked.

'On and off. Mark encourages me. What about you, Dad? Don't you miss it?'

'I do when I see a piano.'

'Do you ever see the others? Are they still playing?'

'I see them from time to time and Bill's always trying to get us back together.'

'Why don't you Dad? Why not get the piano out of store? You've got the room now.' She swivelled round to face him. 'Will you do one thing for me? Will you play at the wedding … with me?'

'I might be a bit rusty.'

'We can practice.' He smiled.

'Of course. What shall we play ...?'

'"When somebody thinks you're wonderful"' they chorused and laughed.

'What about "The way you look tonight"?' Ash suggested.

'Lovely. We could have a practice after tea.'

They sat in companionable silence. Claire pressed up crumbs from the plate with her finger. His daughter was such a pretty woman he thought. Lovely eyes, like her mother.

'Dad, what is Tom going to do?'

'I don't know. What do you think?'

'He feels he can't live up to your expectation,' she said. 'He worries about you – both of you.'

'There's no need.'

'I know he wants to stop drinking but I'm not sure he can.' Ash nodded.

'Thank goodness I never had to worry about you.'

'No,' she said sharply. 'You never did. I longed for you to ask if I was all right but you always jollied me along. You only seemed happy if you thought I was all right – so I tried to be like that.' Ash was shocked.

'But you were the one I didn't have to worry about. The one I didn't feel guilty about. Somehow it seemed to be OK with you. You didn't demand the attention that the others did.'

'I didn't want to worry you,' said Claire.

'Oh Claire, I am so sorry. I just assumed you were OK. I couldn't get it right. Whatever I did, it wasn't enough. I made mistakes. I know that, but I've spent so much of my life, trying to make up for it and somehow I felt you understood.'

'I did, Dad. I knew what you were trying to do but it didn't mean that I didn't need some love and support too.'

'I didn't realise. I'm so sorry. I mistook your calmness for you being OK. The one thing that keeps me going – kept me sane – was that you at least you were all right. I couldn't go on anymore, persecuting myself and always I thought, look at Claire, she's all right. It never occurred to me that you weren't.' Ash reached out, taking her hand, then reached forward to hug her. This little girl who had stood by, allowed the others to have all the attention, withholding her needs. What a precious gift he'd had, right there in front of him, and he had almost overlooked it.

Chapter 52

It was Christmas. As a child it had been the one time when his adoptive parents seemed happy. His Uncle Jack and his girlfriend, who somehow seemed too old to be called that, came for the day and there had been presents. Good ones, like a bike when he was eight and books, and they watched silly television programmes and he would look round, catching Uncle Ted's eye and he'd wink.

He enjoyed buying presents, especially for people he liked. Geraldine was always a nightmare. If she didn't actually say what she wanted, usually expensive and specific, he had to make sure it could be changed – wrong colour, size, purpose.

In spite of this, on Christmas Eve he sat wrapping presents, Christmas music just audible on the telly, a whiskey on the table. This year he would go to church. The church would probably be packed with children and he would enjoy the singing.

He turned the handle and pushed open the heavy door. The atmosphere like old velvet caught his throat. A man handed him a hymnbook and he was pleased to receive a nod and a smile. He made his way to an empty pew near the back of the church. People nodded to him. He sat down and surprised himself by kneeling. With his fingers tight against his forehead, he wished … wished that perhaps here he could find some answers. There was a huge tree decorated with mismatched decorations. How they got the top ones up there? Must have been a ladder job – angel?

'Forgive us our sins … left undone those things we ought to have done…' Was there actually meaning in some of this ritual? He had left undone things he ought to have done. It was tear-making. Could this be somewhere he could turn?

The readings were the familiar Christmas readings and he found surprising comfort in their familiarity. The vicar stepped up to the pulpit and welcomed everyone. Ash sat back, interested now.

'I was in my garden at the weekend,' the vicar began, 'and I saw the concrete-like earth, frosted by the winter and I thought of all the hard work needed to make it into the smooth tilt needed so that I could plant the seeds for my spring vegetables and it made me think of ...' Ash felt a surge of disappointment. The same disappointment he felt if he ever caught a religious programme and was initially seduced into thinking that this representative of God was going to say something revolutionary or challenging. He didn't want homely metaphors, he wanted sturdy robust new thoughts, things he hadn't thought of, couldn't know because he hadn't studied the scripture, things that would uplift him and take his thoughts to a higher plane.

'... marigolds or slug pellets, should I use them or rely on nature?' Ash pressed his eyes shut hard.

'In the name of the Father, the Son and the Holy Ghost'. The man held up his garments, watching his step as he left the pulpit, crossed the chancel and announced the next hymn.

In irritated despair Ash endured the rest of the service, momentarily entranced as a troupe of children sang "Little Jesus Sweetly Sleep" with uncertain tentative voices. A little lad who had talked loudly throughout the service, now sang in the same way, loud and out of tune but with such gusto that the congregation smiled indulgently. He wondered at the obedience of the congregation. Was this enough for them?

When the service ended, the couple in the pew in front turned and smiled at him. Other people nodded and greeted each other. The vicar walked to the door. What would he do if Ash went up to him shook his hand and asked if now could they have an intelligent conversation about religion, life, shame, sin? Would he say 'yes, of course. Let me just finish up here and we can have a talk'. Ash shook the man's hand. Of course, he wouldn't. He would look embarrassed and worried, wondering what he might ask.

The experience had saddened him. This year he was not going home to a Christmas meal filled with a feeling of well-being, duty done. He was filled with emptiness, aware of his nastiness. Where was his compassion? Why did he expect so much? It was only God after all. Wasn't he supposed to be the answer to everything? Was that paltry watered down homes and gardens homily all that this servant could manage? There must be more. Nothing was expected of them. Nothing to make them think.

Chapter 53

'You don't often mention your dad, Brenda,' Ash said.

'I hate him,' said Brenda. 'I wish he was dead.'

'That makes me feel sad.'

'Why?'

'It would have been good for you, if you'd had a dad who could show that he loved you.' Brenda shot a look at him.

'What do you mean?'

'Well, who spent time with you, was interested in you. Did he ever show you any interest?'

'I don't want to talk about it. I just forget it.'

'The trouble is Brenda, that I don't think we do forget these things. I think what happens is that we bury them.'

'OK so I've buried it. It's all in the past.'

'What does that mean Brenda?' She sat, her hair lank today shielding her face. 'It means he can't hurt me now.'

'Hurt you?' Her face, so sad, eyes lost.

'How could he do that? He was like a pimp.' Ash waited. 'He set it up. He knew what Alf was like … and afterwards, when I was upset, he laughed. He laughed at me! He said what did I expect? What did I think Alf wanted? I thought he just wanted to go for a drink. I don't want to think about it.'

'You don't want to think about that horrible time.'

'My dad said there was nothing wrong. It was natural. I'd been leading him on. Always pleased to see him. I was pleased to see anybody. Nobody ever came to our house. I though he was different. But he was just like all men.'

'All men?'

'Well, not you.'

'I am a man.'

'I know … but you're different.'

'Am I?'

Of course. You wouldn't do things like that.'

'You wanted me to.'

'Not like that. Anyway, this is different. I love you.'

'Did you ever love your dad?'

'No … well, maybe once. He was all right when we were little. He used to take Sandra and me to school in his van and we'd sing to the radio and he always stopped at the shop and bought us something and he taught me to ride my bike, but how could he do that?' She paused, staring out of the window. 'He was a good drawer. He could draw animals and people and houses. He was really clever. We always asked him to draw things. He'd do a quick drawing then it was like he got fed up. I used to collect them up. Sometimes Sandra and me coloured them in. He only ever drew with a pen or a pencil. No colour. It was like he didn't know he was good at it. Some people don't do they? Her eyes narrowed. The familiar redness showed on her neck.

'How could he do that? How could a father do that to his daughter? Send her off to be …' Brenda put her head down. She was crying.

They sat in silence, Brenda crying, somewhere else.

Chapter 54

Spring was at last in evidence. The fields ploughed into rich fecundity. It was Ash's weekend to have the dog. It padded along beside him, tail wagging. In the hedgerows tiny, primrose-like flowers had appeared. It was the last week of Leila's placement. Things felt better. Maybe the depression was lifting at last. His driving was confident again. Gone was the tentativeness, stomach jolting at minor negotiations.

Brenda was late, unusual for her. It was three months now since he had started seeing her on her own and so far the sky hadn't fallen down. Chicken Licken. One of Sasha's favourite books. Chicken Licken so afraid that the sky would fall down. Sasha. How infrequently he allowed himself to think about her. On his visits to the cemetery, he talked to her, just able to allow the half an hour conversation, as he weeded the forget-me-knots and pretty pink rose they had planted, but that was all he could bear. One day, when he felt stronger, he would think about her some more. Maybe he would even write about her. Keep it with the photographs. Now, it was just survival. Keep the memories at bay. Manage it. There was a knock on the door and Brenda came in.

'Hello Dr Jones. Sorry I'm late. Jonesie, my cat, brought in a mouse and I thought I'd better get it out before I left.'

'Jonesie? You call your cat Jonesie?'

'Yes.' She smiled. 'I named him after you. He's only a year old.' They looked at each other. Ash smiled. They had moved so far. This was not the obsessive behaviour of a disturbed young woman. This was a gentle acknowledgement. She'd named her cat after him. It felt important.

Chapter 55

Ash woke. The phone was ringing. He glanced at the clock. It was one-twenty. He reached over and picked up the receiver.

'Hello,' he said. 'Hello ... hello.' He replaced the receiver. He pulled the duvet back over himself. Ten minutes later, the phone rang again. He picked it up. 'Hello. Hello.' Again there was no reply. What if it was Tom trying to get him, but this time, he couldn't return to sleep so quickly. He was just dropping off, when it rang again. He sat up and grabbed the receiver. 'Hello. Tom is that you?' He heard a click at the other end of the phone. Now thoroughly awake, he dialled one-four- seven-one. Number withheld, he heard.

He had forgotten about the phone call when he went to bed the next night, until it rang. There was no answer. It was one twenty. It was as if the caller knew the best time to disturb him. He was restless and uncomfortable, and now wide awake, unable to control humiliating and shameful thoughts, familiar and unwelcome. They played round and round in his head, pushing all sensible thoughts aside. Reading was impossible. The phone rang again. He stared at it. The ringing continued, then he heard the answerphone click in. The phone was put down halfway through the message. Logically he told himself that if Tom really needed to talk to him, he could leave a message. But who could it be? Who phones anybody at this time of night? Perhaps somebody had got the wrong number? If it happened again, he would check with them, and hope it didn't further encourage whoever it was.

The next night, he found himself putting off going to bed. He turned off the phone hoping there would be no emergency. Since the business with Tom, he and Geraldine had arranged that they would always be in phone contact. He disconnected the landline and put on his mobile. The only people who knew that number were family, Eva and close friends. He went to bed, more relaxed.

His mobile vibrated on the bedside table. He shot awake. He answered, then noticed the time. It was one twenty. The phone at the other end, clicked off. He was now horribly disturbed. He felt intruded upon and strangely frightened.

His irritable mood had not left him when he turned into the car park. Somebody parked in his usual place, didn't help. He drove round the back. Rosemary was in the office.

'Rosemary. I need to ask you, is there any way my private numbers could have been given out to a patient or somebody outside?' Rosemary looked concerned.

'No, Dr Jones. Everybody knows not to do that. We are very careful.'

'Well, somebody has got hold of my home number.'

'Oh dear. And you think it could be somebody from here. Can't you ask them … ask them to stop?'

'They don't speak, that's the trouble. Just phone and put the phone down.'

'Oh, I see. That does sound worrying. I will check, but I can't think it would have come from here. We are all so careful … everybody understands about it.' He felt further irritated. That didn't seem to be the source, but if not from here, then where had the person got his number?

The next evening he got back at about eleven. It had been a good evening. He was relaxed. He went to bed, aware of possible disturbance, but resigned. He slept through. There was no phone call. The same thing happened the next night. Whoever it was had given up.

A week later, the phone rang at four twenty. In the dark, Ash knocked the receiver onto the floor. He struggled to retrieve it. He'd put the landline back on deciding his night caller had given up. He listened as the answerphone clicked in and heard the caller put the phone down. A sense of sickening despair came over him.

Over the next three nights, the same thing happened. On the third night, he turned all the phones off. He slept relatively well, except that he woke, unprovoked, at around four unable to get back to sleep.

He was struggling not to let it play on his mind. He did not want the paranoia to kick in. Already he was suspecting people. Petri was doing it to undermine him. Ali as a sort of joke, but most likely it was a patient, present or past, and that worried him the most, as he would have no control over that.

A week later Rosemary put her head round the door, propped open against regulations.

'Dr Jones, can I have a word? I've been thinking about your phone calls. They are still happening, are they?' He nodded. 'I am sorry. The thing is ... when did they start?'

'A month or so ago.'

'Yes, well, that's what I wondered. About a month ago I had that very bad cold ... you wouldn't remember. Anyway, I was off for a couple of days and we got in a temp. Usually I am very careful to tell anybody new about security and not to give out private numbers ... but I wasn't here and in the rush ...' Ash smiled.

'I understand.'

'I just wondered,' Rosemary continued, 'if this girl could have given out your number. Anyway, we've used her before, so I contacted her. She was a bit upset – I suppose she felt told off – which she was being, in a sense. Anyway, she is a sensible girl and when she realised I wasn't going to get cross, she said, they had been very busy and she though it was possible she might have given out a number, but she couldn't be sure.'

'Did she remember if it was a man or a woman?'

'No, I asked her that but she said she couldn't actually remember doing it – but that he must have sounded genuine saying he was staff or something and how sorry she was. Sorry, that's not much to go on but I thought I'd better tell you.'

'She referred to the caller as him?' Ash asked.

'Well, yes, but I think that was just in a manner of speaking. I don't think she could really remember.'

'Thank you Rosemary.' At least that was a possibility. It didn't really help but made some sort of sense.

Chapter 56

He was drinking more. He tried to think of positive things. Tom hadn't been in contact. No news is good news, he told himself. Brenda really had turned a corner. His meetings with her were less frequent and they were discussing the possibility of her coming back to the group. Leila was coming to the end of her placement. He still hadn't addressed the business of Brenda with her, but only a fool tells the whole truth, he told himself. He seemed to have a head full of platitudes today. He was though, still plagued with anxious thoughts. He suspected Petri of watching him. Ali was distant. Twice she had asked him to go out for a drink, but he was wary, preferring to be at home. Renée had contacted him to say she was working again but it was Easter and she was going to see her grandchildren in Germany for three weeks. He made understanding noises but felt disappointed and Geraldine constantly reminded him of the nearness of Claire's wedding. He liked Mark and hoped Claire was making the right decision but the preparations seemed exorbitant and Geraldine was doing more than enough for both of them. He would proudly walk Claire down the aisle, probably more full of feelings than he acknowledged but now, which suit he wore and if his shoes matched, he couldn't be bothered with. And, they would be forced into facing the absence. Tom might or might not be there, but Claire's little sister, the would-be-bridesmaid would be absent. He shivered. He could do with a hug. He thought of Eva, but Eva was far away. He needed to make more effort for something to happen. The truth was, he didn't feel in that good a place. He wanted to feel well when he saw her. He didn't know yet, how much vulnerability he could show her.

It was a week since he'd had any phone calls. Once again, he hoped that whoever it was had got tired of the lack of response. In his office, a blue envelope had been put on his desk. His name and address neatly hand written. It must have come with the afternoon post. A branch heavy with blossom, scratch, scratched against the window pane. Ash slit open the envelope. Inside was a newspaper cutting. It was from an obituary section. He glanced at it and froze. Under the heading was his name. Ash Jones.

'Ash Jones 57,' he read, 'died suddenly last week.' He would be fifty seven in a couple of months.

Over the first shock, he read on.

'Ash Jones died suddenly last Thursday. He will be remembered for his sterling work in mental health. He died, characteristically doing what he particularly believed in, running a patient group at the clinic where he had worked for over fifteen years.'

Ash made himself take a breath. 'Those of us who knew Dr Jones may sometimes have wondered about the man behind the kindly mask. It hid a warm, caring man. Turning his back on prestige and financial reward, Ash Jones preferred to work with people not able to afford private fees.'

Ash felt a cold shiver. The use of *us*, suggested it was a colleague or someone who knew him, but what colleague would write this? It seemed much more likely to be a patient and was the writer a man or woman?

'As well as a respected clinician, Ash was also a family man.' Ash raised his eyebrows. 'He leaves a son and daughter and his wife with whom, though separated, he maintained a warm connection.'

Who the hell had written this? 'There was also tragedy in Ash's life. The death of his youngest daughter in a car accident ...' Ash felt his anger rising. He threw the letter on the desk. Who the fuck had written this?

A bit of him wanted to laugh at the sheer audacity but it had shaken him. He held the paper up to the light. It looked like a newspaper cutting but anybody with a bit of computer knowledge could have mocked it up and whoever it was had taken a lot of trouble to find out about him. Could they have done that without knowing him? He put the paper back in the envelope and put it in the desk drawer.

Who was trying to get to him? He needed Renée's common sense, but she wasn't here and he was afraid that late at night, his mind might return to it. He felt very alone. It felt like a test, and not one he felt sure he could pass.

It was a Saturday. He had slept badly but there had been no phone calls. He washed up and forced himself to hoover the sitting room. He picked up two CDs and opened the cupboard drawer. His eye was caught by small box near the back. He picked it up marvelling as always, at its shiny black wood, inlayed with butterflies. His mother's treasure. He took the hatpin out of the box. The silver was a bit tarnished. He rubbed it on his sleeve. He twirled it round in his fingers. Did she wear a hat? He rolled the fluted head in his fingers, feeling the roughness. He pushed the end through the sleeve of his jumper, guiltily, just as he had done as a boy, knowing its sharpness – knowing that if he wanted to he could stab it into something.

He touched the end of the pin with his thumb, and pushed. It hurt. He pushed harder. Pain ran up his arm. He pushed harder. He jerked his thumb away. A spot of blood grew around the pinprick. A surprising amount. He put his thumb to his mouth and sucked. The blood was sweet. He took the hatpin and savagely jabbed it into his thumb again and again making him gasp and screw up his eyes. Several spots of blood sprang out. A vengeful feeling was welling up in him. He pulled some magazines across the table and began jabbing the pin into them, jabbing and tearing. This is all. All that I have of this woman. All I have of her. He was jabbing furiously now. The end of the pin bent, then snapped. Tears started. Ridiculous tears. He sank onto a chair. He'd broken the only thing that remained of his mother.

Chapter 57
Monday

'I told you, several weeks ago, that the appraisals had to be done.' It was Monday morning and as soon as he had arrived Petri caught him. 'Come on Ash. What's going on? I can usually rely on you for this stuff.' Petri looked worried. How small his eyes got when he was angry, Ash noticed. He wonders if I'm cracking up, Ash thought.

'The trust is meeting next week. What do I tell them? I need the stuff on my desk by the end of the week. There's a good chap. Get to it.' Ash felt the usual irritation at being called a good chap but he was shocked. Had he been told?

When he had gone Ash realised he felt very hot and a bit sick. He was shocked at his total lack of recall but that aside, now he had to do them. Pages of attempts to quantify procedure, hugely time consuming and with no therapeutic value. Is that why he'd forgotten? By Wednesday, the end of the week, Petri had said. He thought of his recent pattern; work, home, something to eat, a glass or two of wine and then bed or falling asleep in front of the telly. There had been no phone calls this week, but he knew that might be the caller giving him false hope. His efforts to get the calls blocked had been frustrated by the random timing and need to keep the line open for emergencies. But he had only himself to blame. He hadn't done any work outside of clinical contact, for weeks. He'd had a few evenings out with friends. There was even talk of reforming the band, but he had been fairly reclusive. And now this. Fuck. How could he fit it in?

* * *

The door shut. That was the fourth review he'd done today and it just confirmed for him the stupidity of the exercise. His irritation added to his growing wish to tear the forms up. Fill them in himself. Walk away. He felt a chill. Another of his patterns. His knowledge that if it got too bad, he might just walk away.

At home he poured a whiskey and turned on the television. He put last night's pasta in a dish to re-heat, sprinkled some oregano on a lamb chop and put it in the oven. He went back into the sitting room to watch the news.

The television woke him. A quiz show with loud cheering. He was freezing. The room was dark and the blinds undrawn. He went into the kitchen. He opened the oven door. Clouds of charring smoke hit him and set off the smoke alarm. He threw open the window and waved the air frantically with a tea towel. He re-set the smoke alarm. It was twelve thirty. Had he been asleep all that time? He remembered nothing except sitting down to watch the news. In the sitting room, on the floor the pile of files were scattered where he had probably kicked them. Whatever, they were still not done. Another evening wasted.

He sat, still dazed, watching the late news. He could so easily have caused a fire. Horrific scenes of fighting, bloated corpses and children's terror flashed up on the screen. He watched in numb horror. What had he to complain of? In the kitchen, the air had cleared a little. He shut the window and soberly went to bed.

He dreamt vividly and woke at five. He dressed and spreading the papers out on the table, spent two hours on the reports. By seven he was well into finishing. Getting on with the task had proved to be less arduous that he thought. He even found the statistical comparisons slightly interesting.

He opened the curtain. The sun was shining. The obituary and the phone calls had frightened him, he realised. Now acknowledging this he felt stronger. He had chosen to work with people whose reality was sometimes different. So was his at times. If this person needed to do this, fine, but he need not give them the power of frightening him.

Chapter 58
Ronnie

Ronnie was shouting. 'It isn't fair. I haven't done anything. They've said I've got to leave. I never did anything.'

'Tell us what happened, Ronnie,' Norma said. She looked towards Ash for help.

'I took some biscuits. I was hungry. Alice told them and I've been suspended. Then some money went missing. They said it was me. I take biscuits, not money. What do I want money for? I never go shopping. I've got all I want. I don't need it.'

'Are you sure it wasn't you?' Carl said. Ronnie turned on him.

'What do you mean? I told you. I didn't take the money and now they're going to send me away. I like it where I am.' He looked upset.

'Leave him alone Carl,' said Steph. 'Can't you see he's upset?'

'Yes I know but it's like when I was at Coleman's. I hadn't done anything wrong but they sacked me.'

'Course you'd done something wrong. You'd been looking at that woman's legs.'

'Yes, but that's not criminal,' said Carl.'

Ronnie's large frame filled the chair and he was banging the flat of his hand on the arm of the chair. Ash had never seen Ronnie as threatening, but today he had a glint in his eye that made him look crazed and his hope for a quiet session was clearly not going to happen.

'You're angry and upset Ronnie,' Ash said.

'Of course I'm bloody upset. I bet you've got a nice house and nobody's going to turn you out. I've got nowhere and nobody. Nobody cares about me. You lot don't care.'

'We do,' said Norma.

Was it the words? I've got nobody. Nobody cares. We are all the same, thought Ash. He thinks nobody cares. I think nobody cares. Our circumstances are different but fundamentally, we feel the same. Who is supposed to care? Anybody?

Ronnie was out of his chair and crossing to Carl, who was covering his face with his hands.

'Sit down Ronnie!' Ash commanded. Ronnie towered over Carl, then looked at him, and went back to his seat.

'He called me a liar.'

'Ronnie – tell us again what actually happened. Last week you say you took some biscuits.'

'Yes,' Ronnie looked sullen.

'Then you tell us that you don't need anything. You have everything you want.'

'Yes.'

'So why take the biscuits?'

'I was hungry.'

'But you could buy biscuits. Or ask for them. I'm sure Mrs Bright would have given you some if you'd asked.' Ronnie nodded. 'So why?' said Ash.

'They are a special sort. I don't know where they get them from. My mum used to buy them.'

'So why didn't you tell them that?'

'I felt stupid.'

'I see,' said Ash. 'You wanted these biscuits because you couldn't get them for yourself. What you couldn't do was explain or ask Mrs Bright to get you some. You were able to pay.'

'I didn't like to make a fuss.'

'Right.'

'But taking money is different,' said Steph. Ronnie went to leave his seat.

'I didn't take the money.'

'Stay in your seat, Ronnie,' said Ash. 'Why did they think you took the money?'

'Because of the biscuits. I think I know who took the money but I couldn't say.'

'Why not?' said Norma.

'Because you don't tell on people. Don't you believe me?' said Ronnie, angry again. Ronnie's anger was beginning to worry him. The incident was stupid, almost trivial. Ash was finding it hard to think.

'It doesn't really matter whether we believe you or not,' said Ash, 'but I am asking you, because only you know, did you take the money Ronnie?'

'No,' said Ronnie firmly.

'If that's the truth, then I think you should go and have a straight talk with Mrs Best.'

'Yes, maybe.' They sat in silence. Even Steph looked anxious. Ronnie stared at the floor, then his shoulders seemed to sag and he eased himself back in his chair. Ash noticed his own breathing slowing. Carl shuffled. Steph moved in her chair.

'I didn't mean to call you a liar,' said Carl. 'I just meant I understood what it was like to be accused of something you didn't think you'd done.'

'But I didn't do it.'

'No ... I know.'

'What will happen if Ronnie does get thrown out?' said April. 'Can't you speak to Mrs Best, Dr Jones?'

'Let's see how Ronnie gets on doing it himself. He can tell us next time what happened.'

Chapter 59

The group left the room. Ash felt so weary. He had hardly been able to engage with the business of the stolen money, to understand its importance. Here was a man who'd had such a responsible job, held classified information, reduced to worrying about whether he could have the biscuits he liked, and, he'd got caught up with the story. Now he realised he'd lost sight of why this was so hurtful – hadn't helped Ronnie make the connection with his dismissal from work – the humiliation – the accusation of misconduct. He'd completely missed it. He was losing his touch. Had they sensed his preoccupation? He felt weary and the headache was getting worse. He shut his eyes.

Quicksand sucking him down. 'I can't Dad, I just can't.' Cliff edges. Too close, lurching nearness. 'But it's you I love Dr Jones.' Nothing to hold onto. His chest was aching, his feet leaden. The dogs bayed. Stretching their necks to get him. Already he could imagine the first bite, the tearing of flesh. 'Why did you do it?' Branches flayed in the air. Such noise. He felt the heat of the dogs. Heard their panting breath. 'By the end of the week.' Trees whipping into fury now. 'I can't do it dad'. 'Sasha!' A branch snapped free, hurtled into his face, reeling him sideways.

His head was hurting more now. The pain right behind his eyes, a spasm shot through his temple. His chest felt tight. Arms forward – stretching for the unreachable. He heard a scream.

Brenda had decided to return to the group. She didn't think she would ever tell the group about her feelings for Dr Jones. She would though, tell him her decision on her own, rather than just turning up the next week. She got up early and took the bus. She thought that she could catch him after the group. She could wait until they had all gone. She knew he had a coffee break about then. Brenda knocked on the door. The group had finished, she had been told.

He couldn't breathe.

There was no reply. She turned the handle. Dr Jones was lying on the floor, his eyes closed and his breathing shallow.

Fighting to move forward ... the baying almost on him. Then a hand ... a hand reaching towards him. Strong grasp enclosing his fingers. A last effort – pulling him to safety.

The pain was unbearable. He groaned. Somebody helped him. Put a pillow under his head; ran out to Rosemary; told her quietly, so there wouldn't be a fuss. Turned the 'Do not disturb' sign round; stayed with him till the ambulance arrived.

* * *

Several times she tied to visit but each time people were there. Once a woman who was probably his wife and a young woman who looked like him. His daughter probably. She left quietly. She wouldn't intrude.

Jessica watched as Brenda kept her careful vigil. Knew she wished she could bring him water, bathe his face. Help him eat. Saw Brenda phone the hospital saying she was a friend. They seemed satisfied. She left her number.

'*Can we ever have a relationship?*'
'*You know that isn't possible, Brenda.*'
'*Never? Ever?* she questioned.
'*Never. Ever,*' Ash agreed, '*and you're staying for the group today.*' Brenda smiled and nodded.

The light was dimmed. One day he heard a phone ring. 'No ... not the easiest patient ... we can manage ... thank you ... mental exhaustion'

Chapter 60

Jessica walks along the now familiar street where Brenda lives. She passes the window with the plastic flower and the lemonade bottle and down the hill towards town. On the bus she hardly disturbs the man she sits next to. He touches his face as if brushing away a cobweb. At the square she gets off.

She follows the railing, goes in through the gate, and along the path to the centre of the square. She sits for a moment on a bench, still damp from the overnight rain. Nobody is about except a man walking a small dog on a red lead. From the sky the stallion appears and alights on the grass. Many hands high, its flanks gleam. It waits patiently. Now is the time to say good-bye. One last look. Hooves still. Preparing to leave. Grey-tinged wings. A hand reaches to lift her up. A crack of the whip. Leaves and branches sucked into a glistening vortex, as they leap away.

Chapter 61

Ash walks along the main street, past the shops and the street musicians. The sun is warm. It makes a difference. People smile. He stops to listen to a man making beautiful music with a saw. He drops a coin. How was it that only a month ago, he had felt so bad yet now it was almost impossible to remember how it had been?

The talk had gone well. He feels confident. In control of his subject. The room with its Georgian proportions, tall windows and frescoed ceiling gave a sense of harmony. They broke for coffee. People got up from their seats. Ash looks up and is surprised to see Brenda serving coffee. She looks well. A man from the audience comes up to talk to him. Looking over his shoulder, he sees Brenda talking to a young man. As he turned to go back to his seat, the young man touches her hand. They exchanged a smile. Ash turns his attention to the speaker.

He feels a tap on his shoulder.

'Hello Dr Jones,' says Brenda. She holds out her hand.

Strong grasp enclosing his fingers. Was this the hand that reached out to him, put a pillow under his head, helped him with the pain?

He takes her hand, cool and slim. He meets her eyes. In that moment he knows.

'This is for you.' She smiles, handing him an envelope. Thanking her, he carefully puts it in his pocket and makes his way back to the stage.

It wasn't always the enormity of things that happened that pushed people over the edge, Ash reflected, but the accumulation of sometimes quite small disappointments, sadnesses and humiliations. It still surprised him, the damage to a person if early on they are simply not loved or not loved in a way that nurtures them. On the mantelpiece he places the card that Brenda had given him. Shafts of sunlight cutting through trees into a glade He finds it exquisite. The colours beautiful. In the spare room he's laid out his clothes – on the bed – like old times. He needs to get ready. Taxi will be here soon. He has a wedding to go to.

* * *

Across the rooftops a clock strikes one fifteen. In the half-light a hand brushes some biscuit crumbs from the bedside table onto the floor. It picks up the phone and dials a familiar number.